WITHDRAWN

BUDDY LOVE
Now on Video

BUDDY LOVE
Now on Video

by
ILENE COOPER

■ HarperCollins*Publishers*

Library of Congress Cataloging-in-Publication Data
Cooper, Ilene.
  Buddy Love Now on Video / by Ilene Cooper.
    p.   cm.
  Summary: When Buddy interviews family and friends on videotape, he learns
surprising things about his family and himself.
  ISBN 0-06-024663-4. — ISBN 0-06-024664-2 (lib. bdg.)
  [1. Self-acceptance—Fiction.   2. Family life—Fiction.   3. Interpersonal
relations—Fiction.]   I. Title.
PZ7.C7856Bud   1995   95-1767
[Fic]—dc20   CIP
                                                                            AC

Typography by Christine Hoffman Casarsa
1   2   3   4   5   6   7   8   9   10
❖
First Edition

for W. P.

Chapter One

There were not many things that Buddy Love did well. About this, his parents and teachers agreed.

His lack of achievement puzzled him too. When his mother and father questioned him about why his grades were so . . . so average, he tried to explain. "Nothing has really grabbed me yet."

His father had informed him dryly, "Arranging produce in a grocery store every day doesn't exactly grab me either. It's my job. Yours is to get good grades. Otherwise, you're going to wind up slinging burgers or loading newspapers on a truck, and trust me, Buddy, that's not going to grab you either."

What Buddy didn't tell his father was that actually, there were two things that did interest him immensely—watching television and watching girls. But he didn't see fame and fortune coming from either of those two preoccupations.

Buddy had liked television before he had noticed girls. In fact, his first memories were of watching cartoons on television. He was ashamed to admit it now, but when he was little, he had actually thought that Daffy Duck and Popeye lived inside his television. He spent a lot of time thinking about what they did when he wasn't around.

Now, unlike some of the immature dorks at school, his television taste had traveled far beyond cartoons. Buddy watched everything now, although it was true he didn't watch anything for very long. If there was something that Buddy did do well, it was use the remote control. He was sure he could click faster than anyone else in Chicago.

Click. Click. Click.

Usually, Buddy would race through the fifty-two channels on the cable system, then surf the channels once more, and finally linger over a show that caught his interest. Often, it was a talk show.

Talk shows were the stuff of life. Where else could you learn about family squabbles, the personal lives of celebrities, and, perhaps most important, what men thought about women and women thought about men? As an almost-man himself, Buddy had an insatiable curiosity about that topic.

Why just today, on an afternoon gabfest, three women—a leggy blonde, another blonde with too much hair, and a brunette with glasses—were discussing their boyfriends' bad habits and how they drove the women crazy.

Buddy leaned forward. This could be useful. He was sure he had many bad habits.

"Philip, Philip. Always with the television." His grandmother stood in front of the TV, her hands on her ample hips.

"Oh, Gram," Buddy groaned. "Could you move out of the way?"

His grandmother scowled.

One of the many things that Buddy had learned from television was that grandmothers today didn't like to be thought of as old ladies. Some dressed in jogging suits, some actually jogged, others started their own businesses or dated men young enough to be their sons. Just because women were over a certain age didn't mean they weren't still vibrant and in the Jell-O.

No one had told this to his grandmother, however. She stood blocking the television screen, wearing a shapeless dress similar to the many other faded housedresses hanging in the small closet in the bedroom she shared with his older sister, Sharon. Her socks, one heavy and black, the other a color that seemed to be brown, drooped into shoes so large and boxy that they looked as if they belonged to his dad. Unlike the older women on television, Buddy's grandmother did not wear makeup. Maybe that was a good choice for a face that had so many wrinkles where makeup could lodge. If he hadn't heard his gram yelling when Sharon started using lipstick and mascara, he would have guessed that she didn't even know what makeup was.

Whenever Buddy complained to his parents about his grandmother and her total weirdness, they explained that it was because she came from the Old Country. Since his gram had looked the same age for as long as he could remember, Buddy used to think she came from a country where everyone was old.

He knew now that country was the Soviet Union, at least what used to be the Soviet Union before it had broken up into little countries whose names you couldn't pronounce. They were studying it in Current Events. It hadn't grabbed him.

Behind his grandmother, the girls on *Donahue* were talking about how annoying it was when men left their clothes strewn about. His own mother was always yelling, "Buddy, pick up your stuff or it goes in the garbage can, and you along with it!"

It was interesting to know that women other than his mother found a mess annoying.

"Gram, could you move over, I'm trying to . . ."

"Go outside. Get fresh air."

Buddy lifted his nose and sniffed. "The air in here is okay." He suspected she was far less interested in his receiving the benefits of fresh air than she was concerned about her favorite character on *General Hospital* living through his surgery.

Buddy's grandmother liked two things on television—soap operas and wrestling. Often they watched wrestling together.

Buddy tried once more. "You have a TV in your room."

His grandmother shook her head.

"All right," Buddy said grudgingly. It *was* only a small black-and-white. He got up, and as soon as he did, his grandmother took his place on the couch.

Before Buddy went outside, he stopped and peered at himself in the hall mirror. This event was new in his life. For thirteen years and six months, he had passed this mirror every day, barely noticing it was there. But now, he felt uncomfortable if he didn't take a look before he went outside. Look Before You Leap, an inner voice yelled in his ear, and it was true that the mirror showed him some amazing things.

His eyes, for example. He had heard all his life that they were green like his mother's. But after studying those eyes extremely closely, he knew with certainty only one of them was green. The other had weird brown flecks in it, and though Buddy realized you had to look pretty closely to observe this, he figured eventually someone else would discover it as well. He only hoped it would be a girl who found one green eye and one flecked eye endearing, and not his best friend, Ron, who'd call him a mutant.

He also liked to check the hall mirror to see if any new pimples had appeared within the last hour and a half. Buddy was convinced that pimples always showed up when you weren't looking. Had he been able to maintain a vigilant guard all day, his skin would probably be as smooth as a baby's.

With a bit of trepidation, Buddy approached the mirror. Its brass frame was so tarnished that it seemed the same color as the faded gold flocked paper on the hallway wall. Buddy peered into it.

A ghostly apparition appeared behind him in the mirror. Buddy jumped.

"Oh, it's you," he said, his heart thumping away.

"Who else?" his sister, Sharon, replied with the snarl that she had developed the day she walked into high school and had been successfully perfecting ever since.

"The Pillsbury Doughboy?" Buddy had to step quickly to get out of the way of Sharon's swinging hand. "Well, what *is* all that white stuff on your face?" he continued.

"Rice powder."

7

"Let me get this straight. You have food on your face?"

"Of course not. It's makeup. Women wear it in Japan."

Buddy wanted to remind Sharon she was on the northwest side of Chicago, not Tokyo, but he checked himself.

Sharon leaned into the mirror, just a hint of worry crossing her face. "It's theatrical."

Buddy nodded sagely. "Yeah, like you'd wear in the theater."

"That's where theatrical makeup is usually worn," Sharon said disgustedly.

"No, you can wear it other places. Like the ballet."

Sharon looked at him warily.

"Or television . . . or the circus."

She turned in his direction.

"Clowns. *Very* white faces . . ."

Before she could lunge for him, Buddy threw open the front door and scrambled down the stairs. He was halfway down the block before he looked back, but apparently Sharon felt it would be teen-inappropriate to chase him down the street.

He chuckled to himself. He had really gotten

her this time. He wished he had someone to high-five him. That triumphant feeling lasted about ten seconds. Then, his smile fading, Buddy thought about his sister and her infinite methods of retribution. Perhaps making fun of her face powder wasn't such a hot idea.

It was hard to believe Sharon was a girl. Since he had started to notice girls, really notice them, exactly four months and twelve days ago, he had immediately realized what an endless assortment there was. But no matter how many categories you could divide girls into, Buddy was sure Sharon didn't fit into any of them.

Without squinching his eyes too much, Buddy could see Ron and Zekie standing on the corner two blocks down. Of course, even with his eyes closed, Buddy might have guessed that's where they'd be. Although there was a park just a few steps away, Buddy and his friends hung out on the corner. Sometimes, if there was an actual activity going on, like a ball game, they went inside the park. But usually they didn't bother.

Wishing he had worn his jacket, Buddy buttoned the top button of his shirt. Then he unbuttoned it, even though the late-September afternoon was chilly. He'd look like an idiot with his shirt like that. He didn't know much about fashion, but he knew only mass murderers wore their shirts buttoned at the top.

"Hey," Buddy said, offering the standard neighborhood greeting as he approached his friends.

"Hey," Zekie replied.

Ron was too cool to say Hey. He lifted his hand disdainfully. "What's happening?"

Since Buddy had seen Ron and Zekie barely an hour earlier at school, the answer to that was Nothing. But with Ron especially, he always felt as if something was expected of him. Buddy knew he was not alone in feeling that the reason he existed was to try to impress Ron. If this was actually the case, he might as well stick his head in the oven right now. He had never, to his knowledge, done anything to impress Ron.

For a brief second, Buddy thought he might tell Ron how he had gotten his sister good, but he knew Ron would get that bored look that so easily curtained his face. It wasn't worth it. "Nothing's happening," Buddy conceded.

A girl walked by. She was older, maybe sixteen.

Her bicycle pants and sweater showed off her figure to its best advantage.

"Va-va-va voomski," Zekie said, with a silly grin.

Ron followed Zekie's gaze. "In your dreams, Zekie."

Zekie readily agreed. "I'll say."

Ron looked at Buddy and rolled his eyes.

It was hard to say what made Ron so cool, but he was definitely the kid who everyone wanted to exchange eye rolls with. It made you feel like you were on the inside. Buddy thought about that TV show *Inside Edition*. The announcer always said, "It's a whole different story on the inside." And that was true. On the inside, you were safe, protected. People put up with a lot to feel like that.

The boys rubbed their arms against the growing cold. "Did ya hear about the dance?" Zekie asked.

Buddy nodded.

"A Halloween dance," Ron said with a little snort.

Buddy's heart sank. If Ron decided that the Halloween dance was babyish and refused to go, then probably a lot of other guys wouldn't go either.

"It might be fun," Buddy suggested.

"At school?" Ron said derisively.

"The teachers are gonna get dressed up," Zekie said, excitement coloring his voice.

That was Zekie for you, Buddy thought. He was more excited about seeing old Mrs. Kritz dressed up as a witch, a role she hardly needed a costume for, than the chance to dance with Tiffany Raphael while she was dressed as a harem girl or something.

"I think I'd rather go trick-or-treating," Ron said, smiling. "I like treats . . . and tricks."

"But we've never been to a dance," Buddy said, hoping he wasn't whining.

"We'll go to better dances, Nutty, don't worry about it."

Buddy hated it when Ron called him Nutty. He knew why Ron did it, of course. Just because Buddy hated it. Nutty, Buddy—they were both problematic nicknames and they both came from one dumb movie.

Buddy was not Buddy's real name. He had a perfectly respectable name—Philip. Not a great name, maybe, but not terrible either. Phil had a manly sound.

During his mother's pregnancy, his parents watched an old Jerry Lewis movie on television, *The Nutty Professor.* The professor, Julius Kelp, played by Jerry, was a real nerd. But then the professor created a formula that made him cool—no more buck teeth and bad posture. Instead he was a guy with a sexy deep voice and smooth patter that charmed the ladies. And he changed his name—to Buddy Love. Buddy's dad started calling his yet-to-be-born baby Buddy, and the nickname stuck.

For most of his life, Buddy thought the nickname was okay. Until one day when he was nine, and his parents had rented *The Nutty Professor.*

Buddy sat there appalled. On the screen was an utter dope: Professor Kelp with stringy hair and Coke-bottle glasses. When Kelp turned into Buddy Love, he was better-looking, but mean and obnoxious. Either way, being named for someone in this movie was nothing to be proud of. While his family, even his grandmother, sat laughing around him, Buddy could feel rivulets of sweat rolling down his back. Please, God, he prayed, don't let any other person in the world see this movie.

At that exact moment, the doorbell rang, forever making God suspect in Buddy's eyes. True, it wasn't Ron, but it was Juan, a boy Buddy had never much cared for.

Juan could barely wait until the movie was over to rush to the park and tell the other guys about Buddy's namesake. Unfortunately, Juan didn't speak English all that well. The distinction between Julius Kelp and Buddy Love was lost on him.

Juan did make the guys understand there was a goonbird in a movie, and his name was Buddy Love. He had demonstrated the Nutty Professor's buck-toothed laugh, which several of the kids, including Ron, imitated to perfection. Buddy kept trying to explain that he wasn't the nerdy professor, he was the other half of the split personality, the cool guy, but everyone was too occupied giving Buddy the business to pay attention.

Buddy had a permanent stomachache in the fourth grade. Finally, most of the kids forgot about the whole thing, except when *The Nutty Professor* reared its ugly head on the late movie. Only Ron regularly called him Nutty or Jer or the professor. Buddy always laughed it off, as he did now.

"Yeah, I guess I'd have to be nutty to go to a dance where we might see Mr. Dunlap dressed as a ghost," Buddy said.

That started the boys off on a round of suggestions for their principal's costume. Portly, bald Mr. Dunlap could go as Elmer Fudd, as Buddy suggested; or, Ron said, he could wear a wig and go as Aunt Bea, from *The Andy Griffith Show.* The boys were laughing so hard, they didn't notice that the wind was whipping up.

"Hey, it's freezing," Ron said, even though he was wearing a denim jacket.

"I'm going home," Buddy decided. He usually didn't like to be the first to break up a party, but now he was too cold to care. He sprinted home, hoping that dinner would be on the table soon.

Dinner was served early at the Love home. Mr. Love, who was the produce manager at the local Jewel Food Store, liked to eat, read the newspaper, and get to bed, so he could be at the grocery store first thing when the fresh produce arrived. Eating fashionably late at their house meant six o'clock instead of five.

Since Buddy's mother worked at the library checking out books, it was usually his grandmother who made dinner. From watching cooking shows on television, Buddy knew that a trend in food was something called nouvelle cuisine, small portions of very light food. Like jogging suits, this was a concept with which Buddy's grandmother was not familiar. The words that came to her mind when thinking about food were *big*, *heavy*, and *thick*. Buddy didn't mind; he could eat anything without gaining an ounce. But his sister, who was always on a diet, usually ate about three bites, pushed her plate away, and left the table. That upset his mother, to say nothing of his grandmother, making dinnertime tense. Buddy tried to eat his way through the fights.

By the time Buddy got home, everyone was home and sitting around the table.

"Buddy . . ." his mother began.

"I know. Sorry." He slid into his seat.

Gram started ladling out some of her stew, a dish that let her use all her favorite cooking words.

Sharon stared down at her bowl as if the dumplings were about to jump up and attach themselves directly to her hips.

Mrs. Love cleared her throat. "So, Lou, what happened down at the store today?"

His mom asked his dad that question almost every day, and every day his father just shrugged.

So it was to Buddy's utter and complete amazement that Mr. Love put down his spoon, looked around the table, and said, "There's good news!"

Chapter Two

Good news. Now when was the last time the Love family had received good news, Buddy wondered. On sitcoms, people regularly got good news. Someone was always bagging a promotion or falling in love. Of course, by the first commercial this generally turned into bad news, but before the credits rolled, everything worked out, leading to hugs all around.

His parents, as far as Buddy could tell, liked life to be as devoid of news as possible. "No news is good news," he often heard his mother say. She especially said it when she was riffling through the mail and found no bills or letters from relatives. Buddy thought this attitude was extremely boring and had vowed to have plenty of news in his life. He looked at his father expectantly.

"I won a video camera," Mr. Love said.

This news was met with a mixed reaction. Mrs. Love disappointedly murmured, "Oh. I thought it might be a raise." Sharon, staring off into space, seemed not to have heard, while Gram just looked puzzled. Since she had only a nodding acquaintance with the Mixmaster, the microwave, and the dishwasher, preferring to use her egg-beater, her stove, and her hands, Buddy was sure she didn't have the faintest idea what a video camera was. Buddy, on the other hand, was delighted.

"That's great!" he said, trying to make up for the lack of enthusiasm being shown by the rest of the family.

"What are we going to do with it?" Mrs. Love asked.

"Well, Ann," Mr. Love said, with just a touch of exasperation, "we'll do what the rest of the world does with 'em. Film family events."

That brought a moment of contemplative silence to the table.

"If the kids were younger . . ." Mrs. Love began.

Sharon came to life. "Oh, excuse me. Now that we're old, ugly teenagers, instead of sweet, drooling babies, I guess there's no point in recording us."

"Speak for yourself, Dogface," Buddy interjected.

"Hey, hey." Mr. Love slapped the table.

"I just meant maybe we should sell it," Mrs. Love continued.

Buddy groaned. Wasn't that just like his parents? An unexpected gift arrives, a wonderful gift, and what do they want to do? Get rid of it before it even enters the house.

"I hadn't thought of that," Mr. Love said, considering.

"Dad, please. It would be great to have a camcorder. We could take it to the park and up to the lake . . ." Buddy tried desperately to think of other places they might use it. Then he had a brainstorm. The one thing his father actually had a passion for was the Chicago Bears. Tickets to the game were expensive, so they didn't go very often, but the team's summer training camp was held in a northern suburb, and anyone could come out and watch the Bears practice. "We could take the camera up to Lake Forest and tape the Bears."

Mr. Love's mouth relaxed into a smile. "Now there's a thought."

"That would be so cool," Buddy continued excitedly. "You get off of work early, so we could be up there most of the afternoon. Then we could ask Ron and Zekie and some of your friends to come over and watch the tape. Maybe even have a barbecue."

"Oh, that sounds like fun," Sharon remarked, each word dripping blood.

Buddy turned to her. "Here's something else we could use a camcorder for. We could tape you going to the Junior Prom. Of course, if by some chance you're not invited, we could tape you all pathetic, in those torn flannel pajamas of yours, crawling into bed at eight o'clock, just when everyone else is hitting the dance floor. . . ."

"Buddy!" His mother glared at him.

"Okay, okay." There was no point in losing the momentum on the camcorder just to taunt his sister. But by the time Buddy had that thought, it was already too late.

"That shows you what you know." Sharon was

getting up a head of steam. "It so happens I have a date for this Saturday night."

The camera disappeared like the flame on a birthday candle. Sharon and her date were now the topic under discussion.

"With who?" Mrs. Love asked, eyes narrowed.

"You don't know him," Sharon replied airily, making it clear this was definitely a point in the boy's favor.

"Well, we're going to get to know him, aren't we?" Mr. Love demanded. "He's picking you up, isn't he?"

Sharon made a face. "Oh, Dad, you're not going to do that come-in-and-shake-my-hand thing, are you? That's right out of the Stone Age."

"I believe in the Stone Age the father hit the kid over the head with a club if he didn't like him," Mr. Love replied.

"Of course he'll come in," Mrs. Love said hurriedly. "What's his name, Sharon?"

"Dan Walters."

"You mean Danny Walnut?" Buddy asked. He turned to his parents. "The kids call him that because he has the brains of a walnut. Same cracks down the sides of his face, too."

"Was he in an accident?" Gram asked, concerned.

"He was not in an accident, and he's smarter than you, you aspiring moron!" Sharon threw her napkin down on the table and ran out of the room.

Buddy turned back to his father. "So you never said, how did you win the camcorder?"

"Mrs. Kaposki."

"You're kidding!"

Mr. Love had told the family many times about the annoying Mrs. Kaposki, one of the checkout clerks, who was always trying to sell him a chocolate bar or a raffle ticket to raise money for her son's Cub Scout troop or baseball team. Mr. Love was known to sneak into the men's bathroom if he saw her coming, just to avoid handing over more cash.

"The top prize was a trip to London."

Gram made her own peculiar sound, somewhere between a sneer and a snort. "Fah. London. Big deal, big shmeal."

Buddy turned to her. "What's wrong with London?"

"What do they got that we don't got?" she

demanded. Gram was nothing if not a loyal American. Russia, England, they were all the same to her. Old Countries.

"They have a queen," Buddy suggested.

"Fah."

"So the camera was second prize?" Mrs. Love asked her husband.

"Third. We also missed out on a motorbike."

"I prefer the video camera," Mrs. Love said.

"You know, Mom, *camcorder* is really the correct term," Buddy informed her.

"Thank you," she said sulkily.

"So when are we going to pick it up?" Buddy asked.

"How about Saturday?" Mr. Love suggested, turning back to his stew.

"All right!"

Buddy immediately started making plans in his head about what he'd do with the camcorder. Sure, they could go tape the Bears, but that wasn't until next summer. He wanted to tape stuff now. Maybe one day he'd be a famous television director, so he needed to get started right away. He couldn't wait to tell Ron. Not about being a TV director, of course. Ron would just laugh at that. But he could tell him about the camcorder. Finally, he had something that Ron didn't.

The next morning, Buddy jumped into his clothes. When he came downstairs, he saw that Sharon and his grandmother were the only ones left at the kitchen table.

"Look what she's drinking," Gram said, her nose wrinkled in disgust.

Buddy peered into the cup. He didn't want to say what the thin, yellowish liquid resembled. He looked at his grandmother inquiringly.

"Lemon juice and hot water. She thinks that is breakfast."

"Sounds yummy. Can I have eggs, Gram? And toast?"

His grandmother nodded approvingly. "And bacon."

Buddy shrugged. "Okay." He didn't mind eating Sharon's share of the grub. "So why are you drinking lemon and water?" he asked his sister. "Is that how you keep your personality so sour?"

"It's good for the whole system," she muttered.

Buddy was puzzled. "You mean like the solar system?"

"No. My system. It cleanses."

Exactly how it did its cleansing, Buddy didn't want to find out. "Okay," he said agreeably. "More real food for me."

"Bacon and eggs." Sharon's laugh was short and harsh. "And butter on your toast, I suppose. You'll probably keel over from a heart attack by the time you're fifteen."

"I'll worry about it when I hit fourteen."

"What about your complexion?"

Now Sharon had hit a nerve. "What about it?"

"How do you think pimples get started? First, you ingest large quantities of grease. All that excess oil lodges under your skin, primarily in the facial area. With no place else to go, it *pushes*, pushes up, becoming giant pustules . . ."

"All right, all right. Gram," he said, "I don't have time for breakfast after all."

His grandmother turned away from the stove. "It's almost ready," she said.

"You eat it," Buddy said, getting up.

"Wise choice," Sharon said, smirking.

Buddy was tempted to sit right back down, but visions of red eruptions danced through his head. It wasn't worth it. He grabbed his books and jacket and stomped out of the kitchen.

Once he was outside, Buddy looked at the small brick house next door. Since the second grade, and up until the end of last year, he had always stopped to pick up Amy Cudahay. Along the way they had very interesting talks that ranged from the pennant chances of the Chicago Cubs to the trouble with mothers.

This year, Buddy had decided he couldn't take the chance of being seen anywhere in the vicinity of Amy. Last June something bad had happened to her. She had become an outcast.

Buddy wasn't sure how this had come about. The girls were in charge of deciding who was an outcast and who wasn't. The boys didn't have any say in the matter at all. And those girls, they could decide so darn fast. One day, a girl was perfectly all right, in the middle of all the giggles and whispers and that other stuff girls did. The next day, she was off by herself like a piece of stinky cheese. That's what happened to Amy. Buddy never did find out what Amy's crime was, but one day she was history, and it was soon clear that the only way to avoid becoming history himself was to stay far away from Amy.

Amy went to summer camp immediately after school let out and didn't reappear until Labor Day. Buddy felt lousy the first day of school, but he couldn't force himself to stop by her house. It was a chicken thing to do, he knew, but he couldn't take the chance. Buddy pretended not to notice the hurt look in Amy's eyes whenever they accidently exchanged glances.

Buddy always tried to leave for school after he was sure Amy had already gone. But today he'd skipped breakfast, and now there she was, pulling at her door, making sure it was locked. "Oh, heck," Buddy muttered. Amy was looking right at him. For a second, she looked as though she was going to run back into the house, then she turned purposefully in his direction.

"Well, hello," she called. "If it isn't the coward of Coolidge Street."

"Aw, Amy . . ."

"You better hurry up and get to school. You might get spotted talking to me."

Buddy, as he so often did lately, felt confused. Should he boldly walk Amy to school? Or should he hightail it out of here? Amy made his decision easy.

"Don't just stand there. I don't want to be seen with you any more than you want to be seen with me." She raised her voice. "Git!"

Buddy got. He didn't feel good about it, but he picked up steam and didn't look back.

For once in his life, Buddy was early for school. Instead of hanging around the school yard, waiting for his friends to show up, Buddy decided to go to his homeroom. He didn't feel like telling Ron and the other guys about the camcorder now. Seeing Amy had made the day seem even grayer than the cloudy sky.

His homeroom seemed empty at first. Then Buddy noticed Miss Danardo, his teacher, partially hidden behind the closet door, rummaging around inside.

Most guys were interested in women's fronts. But there was something about Miss Danardo's back that gave Buddy the shivers. The whole back part, from her dark hair, caught in a gold barrette, all the way down to her high, high heels.

She turned, saw him standing in the doorway, and smiled. "Good morning, Philip." Now the sun was peeking out a little. "You're early."

Wildly, Buddy sought a witty response to that.

There didn't seem to be one.

"As long as you're here, can you give me a hand?"

"Sure." Buddy hurried toward her, hitting his knee against a desk. Manfully, he bit his lip.

"I'm trying to find a box of chalk," she said. "You know how short of supplies we are. I tucked away an extra box last year," she confided. "Now I can't find it."

Buddy didn't really hear about the chalk. He was too busy breathing in Miss Danardo's perfume. One part of him was breathing. Another part was jumping up and down saying, "You are close enough to be smelling Miss Danardo's perfume." He felt like high-fiving himself.

". . . could you?"

Could he ever! But what was it she wanted him to do?

They looked at each other blankly for a moment. Finally, Miss Danardo said, "My back is bothering me."

"Your back?" That great-looking back hurting? She didn't want him to rub it, did she?

"So if you could reach up to the top shelf and look for the chalk . . ."

Buddy sprang into action now that he knew what was required of him. He found the box, reached back, got it off the shelf, and handed it to her.

"Thank you," she said with a grateful smile.

Buddy wanted to say something that would make the moment last. Something Miss Danardo would remember. "Uh, Miss Danardo, do you ever watch *Oprah*?"

"No. We're in school when it's on."

"They rerun it at four thirty in the morning. If there's a really good show, and, like, you don't hear about it until you get home, you can still tape it," he informed her.

Miss Danardo smiled. "Really? Thank you, Philip. That's good to know."

Buddy went back to his seat a happy man. He felt like he and Miss Danardo had really connected.

Chapter Three

Buddy looked over at his father, who was intent on the traffic. Should he try to talk? He and his dad were hardly ever alone together; maybe they should be bonding.

Buddy cleared his throat. "How long do you think it will take us to figure out the camcorder?"

Mr. Love glanced over at Buddy. "I was hoping you would do that."

"Me?" Buddy asked in surprise. Other than his prowess with the remote control, Buddy was a real fumble fingers when it came to anything mechanical. He once tried to fix a flat tire on his bike and had wound up with a wheel, rim, and screws all over the driveway, much to the amusement of

Ron, who happened to be wandering by, of course.

"You were the one who was so hot to have the thing," Mr. Love said. "I don't have time to figure it out."

Buddy glanced down at the cardboard box he was holding so carefully on his lap. There was a picture on the top of a father smiling as he video-taped his family opening their presents around the Christmas tree. That father had the time to figure it out. Buddy sighed. "I can do it."

"Okay," Mr. Love said, nodding. "Then I'll learn it eventually."

For a moment, Buddy was angry. His dad sure made bonding hard. Didn't he know fathers and sons were supposed to do things together? Heck, that had been going on since *Father Knows Best* was on in prime time. Then, just as quickly as it had flared up, Buddy's anger faded. If his dad wasn't interested in the camcorder, he'd have a lock on it.

As soon as he got home, Buddy took the box upstairs to his room. There was just about space for the two of them. Buddy's room was the smallest in the house, maybe in the world, he sometimes thought, but he knew he shouldn't complain. Sharon had the larger room, but she did, after all, have to share it with Gram.

How many times had she complained to Mrs. Love about the humiliation of it all?

"I ask somebody up to my room and there are Gram's gigantic panties laying on the bed."

"Better than Gram laying on the bed," Buddy had commented.

"That's lying," Mrs. Love had said with a sigh.

"It is not!" Sharon shrieked. "Go look up there right now. There are nightgowns and panties and something she calls a corset . . ."

"I wasn't disputing you; I was correcting your grammar."

"Oh, sure." Sharon lowered the decibel level but added five drops of bitterness. "Worry about grammar, while I become a friendless freak. I might as well be living in a nursing home."

Buddy cocked his ear toward Sharon's room. She didn't sound like a friendless freak now. There were giggles coming from her room. He put down the box—if the truth be told, he was glad to have a reason not to try to puzzle it out immediately— and went to investigate.

Quietly, he crept toward Sharon's room and peeked in.

Sitting on Sharon's bed was the most beautiful girl he had ever seen. Buddy was sure that she had never been around before. He'd have remembered. Even though the girl was sitting down, he could tell she was tall. Her hair was almost silver-blond, and it hung below her shoulders. He couldn't see what color her eyes were, but they were like cat's eyes, and her lips were a nice shade of appley red. As for the rest of her—Buddy tried very hard to get a good look at the rest of her—she seemed to be built like the girls in the magazines that he kept hidden under his bed.

"You have to watch out for Danny," the girl was saying. "He's got Roman hands and Russian fingers."

What did that mean? Buddy wondered. As far as he knew, old Danny Walnut was born in Chicago.

"I can handle him," Sharon said confidently.

The girl just ran a hand through her hair. Buddy would have liked to look at the girl forever, but he was afraid he'd get caught. He stepped backward, and in the process managed to knock a large picture of his dead grandfather off the wall.

"Who's there?" Sharon asked sharply.

Buddy tried to hightail it back to his room, but Sharon stepped into the hall.

"You were spying on us," she accused him.

"Was not." He tried unsuccessfully to put the picture back up.

The Girl, as Buddy now thought of her, came up behind Sharon. "Who's this?"

"Unfortunately, he's my brother."

Now Buddy was able to get a better look. If possible, she was even prettier than he had thought at first, especially with that smile on her face. A smile that, unbelievably, seemed to be directed at him.

"Hey, brother," she said in her lilting voice.

After a few seconds of searching, Buddy found his voice. "I'm Buddy."

"I'm Estella. What are you going to do with that picture?" She nodded at the bulky frame he was still trying to get a grip on.

"Put it down," he said, doing just that.

"Buddy, get lost," Sharon instructed.

"I've got stuff to do," Buddy said, trying to

sound dignified. "Dad wants me to figure out how to work the camcorder."

"Oh, you've got a new camcorder?" Estella asked with interest.

"My dad won it," Sharon told her. "So go figure it out, Buddy."

"What are you going to film?" Estella asked.

"Tape," he corrected.

"What are you going to tape?"

"I haven't decided yet."

"He's going to tape the fungus growing on the dirty plates he keeps in his room. C'mon, I want to show you what I'm wearing tonight." Sharon tugged at Estella's arm.

" 'Bye, Buddy," Estella said, her mouth turning up in what seemed to be an apologetic smile.

The door slammed behind them.

Buddy left the picture leaning against the wall and made his way back to his bedroom. Here, in his tiny cell, it seemed impossible to believe that such a beautiful creature was only steps away. True, she was locked behind a door with his dragon-faced sister guarding her, but she was there, and she had smiled at him.

Buddy stretched out on his bed. His giddiness

wasn't too different from the way he felt when he was close to Miss Danardo, but despite her charms, Miss Danardo was, after all, an adult. Estella was a girl. Only a few years older than himself. Well within his grasp. And she had smiled at him.

Buddy looked at the box with the camcorder waiting patiently to be opened. He didn't see how he could fill his head with fast-forwards and rewinds when it was already full of Estella. But then a thought hit him. Estella had seemed very interested in the camcorder. If he figured out how to work it, maybe he could teach her how to use it. He'd rather bond with Estella than with his dad any day.

With renewed fervor, Buddy sat up and picked up the box. He tried to rip the top off, but it wasn't that easy. For a moment, Buddy despaired. If he couldn't figure out how to open the darn box, was he actually going to be able to work the thing?

Finally, with one giant yank, the box came open. Nestled in Styrofoam was the black camcorder. It looked forbidding. Buddy picked it up cautiously and turned it around in his hands. It wasn't one of the newer, lightweight models. His dad couldn't be that lucky. But despite its bulk, it wasn't too hard to handle. He found the viewfinder and looked through it. He saw his pajamas in a heap on the floor.

Putting down the camcorder, he found the directions and began to read. It was like they were written in another language. He quickly realized that they *were* written in another language—French. He turned to another page and found the English directions. They weren't much easier to figure out.

He struggled with them for another half hour or so, but he didn't make progress. He had identified the on/off switch, the lens, and the microphone, but he didn't have a clear idea of how any of it worked. He was still fiddling with the machine when his mother appeared at the door.

"So how's it going?" she asked.

Buddy shrugged helplessly.

She thrust a book at him. "I brought this from the library."

He took it and read the title: *Fun with Video.* He flipped through the pages and saw nice, clear pictures and diagrams. "Gee, thanks, Mom."

His mother, who wasn't one to show much enthusiasm, nodded and turned to leave.

"Hey, Mom?"

"Yes?"

"Sharon has a friend over."

"So?"

"Do you know her? Her name's Estella."

"I think she moved here at the beginning of the school year."

Where was here exactly? Buddy didn't know how to ask more, but his mother seemed to understand what he was getting at.

"She lives in that brick house at the corner of Waverly and Lotus. I believe her mother is a nurse. I don't think her father lives with them." She smiled and shrugged. "That's all I know."

"I was just curious," Buddy said, a little defensively. Sheesh. Couldn't he take an interest in Sharon's friends for a change, without his mother practically smirking at him?

"Sorry." The smile became pencil thin. "Let me know when you figure out the camcorder. I have an idea about what we could use it for."

"What?"

"I'm going to be making one of my sweet

potato pies this afternoon, and I thought you could tape it."

"Why don't we just take a picture of it?"

"Don't be silly. Tape me preparing it."

Buddy thought this was only slightly less silly. "But, Mom, no one wants to watch a tape of you making a pie."

"Aunt Fan does," his mother responded promptly.

Aunt Fan was his mother's twin sister. They were Ann and Fan, but the resemblance stopped with their names. His mother was straight and thin, almost bony. Tight little curls framed a long, narrow face that looked a lot like Buddy's. Everything about Aunt Fan was round. Huge, blue eyes, a mouth drawn into a cupid's bow, and big everything else. She always wore tightly belted dresses that made her look like a pillow tied in the middle.

"She can't seem to follow the recipe for my sweet potato pie, so I thought maybe if you videotaped the actual preparation, I could send it to Fan as a birthday present."

Buddy wasn't sure why adults wanted presents at all; they never got anything very interesting.

But a tape of a pie being made? His mother would be better off sending Aunt Fan her usual present, five pairs of queen-size pantyhose.

"So what do you think?" His mother looked at Buddy expectantly.

He shrugged. "Sure. But it might take me a while before I'm actually ready to tape."

"I'll wait," Mrs. Love said brightly.

Alone once more, Buddy listened for sounds coming from his sister's room, but it was quiet now. Maybe Estella had left while he was talking to his mother. He didn't think it would be wise to check.

Determinedly, he picked up the book his mother had left for him. The first page began, "Family life is filled with so many moments to treasure. . . ." He skipped over to a section headed "Camcorder Basics."

To his surprise, the instructions began to make sense. He was able to pick out the special features, and he figured out how to load the camera with a cassette. Buddy could feel his heart pounding. He was going to be able to work this sucker.

After reading a little more, just to make sure, he bounded down the stairs, the camcorder under his arm. "Hey, Mom," he called, "got those sweet potatoes cooking?"

She poked her head out of the kitchen. "You mean you're ready?"

"I think so."

"Oh, then I want to change." She threw off her apron and went upstairs.

Buddy went over to the bookshelf where they kept the old videotapes that they planned to watch someday. There were all sorts of things there: movies, soap operas, and old four-thirty-A.M. *Oprah*s. All the Loves agreed that they should recycle the tapes, but each member of the family was afraid the one show he or she wanted, languishing on some unlabeled tape, would be erased. Gram was particularly worried about the *World Wrestling Championship*.

Finally, Buddy just grabbed one. He hoped it had his sister's *All My Children* shows on it.

Buddy was just about to pop in the tape when the doorbell rang. He put the camcorder down on the couch and opened the door to Ron.

"Hey," Ron said, walking in, "I thought you were going to be at the park this afternoon."

This was the moment Buddy had been waiting

for. It had been difficult, but he hadn't told Ron about the camcorder. He was waiting to spring it on him, just like this.

"Oh, I got busy." Buddy was trying so hard to make his voice casual, his throat hurt. "Figuring out my new camcorder."

Trust Ron. He was so cool, his eyelids didn't even flicker.

"Yeah? Where did you get it?"

"My dad won it in a raffle."

"Won it?" Ron shook his head. "Too bad."

"What do you mean?"

"Well, if you win something, you can't pick it out. You just gotta take what they give you. If you buy something, you can get whatever you want."

"But it was free."

"You know what they say. You get what you pay for."

How did Ron do it? In five seconds he had managed to turn winning a camcorder into a pathetic accident. Well this time, Buddy wasn't going to fold. Maybe he wasn't great at standing up for himself, but he was going to stand up for his camcorder.

"It's terrific," he said, picking the machine up from the couch and cradling it in his arms.

Ron looked it over. "It's one of those big ones. Looks like a model that's a couple of years old, maybe more. They have small ones now that are really light. You'll get a hernia lugging that thing around."

"But this size takes a regular cassette like you use in a VCR," Buddy argued. He awkwardly stuck out a hand with the tape still in it. "I'm ready to start taping right now."

"Taping what?"

Buddy's heart sank like a stone. Start taping my mother making a sweet potato pie. There was an impressive television debut. Suddenly, one thing was clear. He was going to have to get Ron out of the house before his mother came flouncing down in her new apron, or he'd never hear the end of it.

"I'm going to tape whatever I feel like," Buddy said defiantly.

"Hey calm down, Nutty. I'm sure there's all sorts of great possibilities around here, like your grandmother drinking a cup of tea or your dad snoozing while he reads the paper."

Ron didn't know how close he was, Buddy thought grimly.

Ron sat down in Mr. Love's easy chair.

"What are you doing?" Buddy almost yelled.

"Sitting," Ron replied, puzzled.

"Well, you can't."

Ron smelled a rat. "Why not?"

Buddy forced himself to calm down. If Ron sensed that Buddy wanted him out of the house, he'd never leave. He was making himself more comfortable every second.

Buddy put down the camcorder. "My mother's having company."

"So let's go up to your room."

"No. I have to be here."

Ron smiled slowly. "Oh, I get it. You're going to be taping some family reunion. Is that Cousin Harold of yours coming? The guy who's always passing gas? Too bad you can't tape in smell-o-vision."

"A lawyer's coming," Buddy improvised. "He's going to be reading a will. Some great-aunt of mine died and we were left money. So I'm going to tape the proceedings."

"No way."

"Way, Ron. You've gotta go."

Ron looked unsure as to whether to believe

this or not, but he got up anyway. Just when Buddy thought he was going to be able to shove Ron out the door, Mrs. Love walked down the stairs. Ron smiled at Buddy evilly.

"Hello, Mrs. Love," Ron said politely.

What a suck-up, Buddy thought.

"Hello." Mrs. Love was cool. She didn't like Ron very much because, she said, he led Buddy around by the nose.

"I guess you're all dressed up for the big will reading."

Buddy closed his eyes.

"The will reading?"

"Yeah, Buddy says he's gonna tape the lawyer telling your relatives who gets what." Ron winked at Buddy.

Mrs. Love hesitated just for a second, then nodded. "Yes. We're lucky Buddy figured out how to work the camcorder so quickly. This is some-thing we definitely want to have on tape. Who knows? Aunt Sylvia may hit Cousin Harold over the head with her walking stick if she doesn't get what she thinks she's entitled to."

Mouth agape, Buddy stared at his mother.

"I'm sorry you can't stay, Ron," she continued,

maneuvering him toward the door. "But this is for family only. You understand."

"Sure," Ron said uncertainly. "Can I see the tape, though?"

"No. Good-bye, Ron." She slammed the door behind him.

Buddy wanted to hug his mom, just like he had when he was a little boy and she saved him from an unfriendly neighborhood dog. But all he said was "Thanks."

"I enjoyed wiping that self-satisfied smile off his face," Mrs. Love said, heading for the kitchen. "I wish you'd get some new friends."

She had been saying that since Buddy was in the fourth grade.

"Now, I thought I'd lay all the ingredients out on the table and you could film them individually before we went into the actual cooking part," Mrs. Love began.

Buddy knew he owed his mother big, but even his gratitude wasn't enough inspiration to make the pie baking interesting. Then he had a flash of that big, tall woman with the goofy voice who did that cooking show on TV. What was her name? Julia Child.

"Hey, Mom, you've watched that Julia Child show, right?"

"I guess I've seen it a few times."

"Well, I think that's how you ought to act in this tape."

"What do you mean?"

"You know, swing your knife around and keep taking sips of wine."

"Buddy, neither knives nor wine are required for this recipe."

"But we could make this tape really funny . . ."

His first foray into directing wasn't going too well. Mrs. Love was glaring at him.

"Buddy, I'm nervous enough about this. I don't want to have to worry about doing a Julia Child imitation."

Buddy was defeated. "Okay, we'll do it straight."

As it turned out, the video was unintentionally funny. Mrs. Love had laid her ingredients neatly on the table, but she seemed to have no idea of how much of anything to put in.

"Now, the salt . . ." she said, smiling inanely at the camera. "Just a pinch. Next pour a little bit of the condensed milk into the batter."

"How much?" Buddy whispered, off camera.

"Oh, just a little. Not too much." She put down the milk. "Now, let me see. Does the sugar come next? I guess it doesn't matter."

By the time the pie mixture was all done, Buddy was thoroughly confused, and he was sure Aunt Fan would be too.

"Now I'm going to bake it," Mrs. Love announced, taking the pie over to the oven. "I've preheated the oven to three hundred twenty-five degrees."

Finally, something definite. "Now, how long do you bake it?" he asked.

For a second, Mrs. Love looked blank. "Until it's done."

"When's that?"

"I'm not sure," she replied helplessly. "I just look at it, and when it looks right it's done."

Buddy shut off the camcorder. Happy Birthday, Aunt Fan.

Chapter Four

Buddy went to his locker to get his lunch. The school lunchroom didn't serve real food, just milk and limp salads and sandwiches that all had something brownish stuck between two pieces of bread.

Mrs. Love had told Buddy that if he didn't want to buy his lunch, either he could make his own or his grandmother would fix it for him. Gram's idea of lunch was two or three large Tupperware containers full of leftovers, so every day Buddy stuffed the same thing into a paper bag: a hunk of cheese, a bag of chips, and an apple. His friends made fun of him, but Buddy didn't care. He was proud of himself for streamlining his midday meal.

He arrived at the usual lunch table where Ron, Zekie, and two other guys, Dave and Joe, were sitting. The subject under discussion seemed to be the Halloween dance.

"No costumes," Dave was insisting.

"They won't be able to tell the difference on you," Ron informed him.

Buddy slid into his seat. "You mean we're going to the Halloween dance after all?"

"Yeah," Ron said, slurping his cola.

Buddy wanted to ask why Ron had changed his mind, but he knew all too well that if he asked such a straightforward question, he'd never get an answer. He'd have to worm it out of Ron, but he had years of experience to help him.

Buddy pulled his cheese out of his bag. "So, costumes or not?"

Ron shrugged. "Why not? You can go as a rat, with all that cheese you eat."

"What about you?"

Ron considered. "Maybe Dracula."

A good choice, Buddy thought privately, Ron's teeth were a little on the pointy side. Not that anyone would actually mention that out loud. Since it didn't seem to be the idea of getting dressed up that had changed Ron's feelings about the dance, Buddy switched directions.

"I guess the girls will all wear costumes," Buddy said, swallowing a bite of cheese.

"Oh yeah, they're all excited about getting dressed up," Ron confirmed. "Tiffany is going as Madonna."

That was it. Ron would never be so uncool as to admit he actually liked a girl, but even he couldn't hide the little smile playing around his lips as he visualized Tiffany as the Material Girl.

"Hey, she isn't going to wear a leather bra or anything, is she?" Buddy asked.

"Sometimes Madonna wears a lot less than that." Ron snickered.

All the boys turned around to look at Tiffany, then looked away.

"It's a school dance," Dave said, shoveling some chips into his mouth. "She'll probably throw a couple of crosses around her neck, and that'll be her costume."

"She said she'd let me help her pick her outfit," Ron told them.

Aha, Buddy thought. Now this was really coming into focus.

"Since when is Tiffany Raphael friends with you?" Joe asked in as close to a rude tone as anyone dared to use with Ron. "She goes for the brain power, like Sammy Mantenga."

Ron crumpled up his napkin and tossed it in the garbage. Bright, slight Sammy Mantenga, whose arm was about the size of one of Ron's fingers, wouldn't have fared much better.

"She's seen the light."

Buddy pondered this phrase for a moment. But he was having a tough time processing the thought that Tiffany Raphael, a girl whose sweaters and socks always matched, and who lived in the biggest house in the neighborhood, and who had been number one in everything since the first grade, had seen a big, bright light shining in her face, and it turned out to be Ron Novak.

Buddy bit morosely into his cheese. Sure Ron had been the leader of the boys forever, and sure, he bragged about his success with girls, especially girls up in Michigan where the Novaks spent the summer—girls no one could ever check on. But now it seemed as if Ron was going to start in on the girls here, and who was the first to fall into line; who was going to wear a leather bra for him, maybe? None other than Tiffany Raphael.

Buddy finished his lunch, but his cheese didn't taste as good as it usually did. He was glad to leave the lunchroom and go back to class, where the sight of Miss Danardo working busily at her desk made him feel a little better.

When the bell rang, Miss Danardo put down her pen and smiled at her students. "Class, I think you're going to enjoy our social studies project."

Buddy doubted it. He was willing to give Miss Danardo's social studies project a chance, but if he enjoyed this one, it would be a first.

"As you know," she continued, "later in the semester we'll be studying the history of our city and our state, but I thought it would be fun to start with something a little closer to home. For the next month or so, I'd like you to explore your own histories."

Well, that wouldn't take long, Buddy thought. He had lived in the same house his whole life, seen the same people, even watched a lot of the same television shows. He hoped that Miss Danardo wasn't going to want more than a page or two for this project.

"I'd like you to talk to your family, find out

where they came from, what their lives were like when they were your age. Ask them what you were like when you were young. You could talk to your friends too, and see what they remember about you. You'll wind up with a picture of yourself you might not have been able to get in any other way."

The word *picture* rang in Buddy's head. He raised his hand. "Miss Danardo?"

"Yes, Philip?"

"Does this have to be a written report?"

"What else were you thinking of?" she asked.

"I just got a new camcorder." He resisted looking in Ron's direction. "Maybe I could videotape the interviews."

Miss Danardo practically clapped her hands. "Why, that's a terrific idea, Philip. Very creative." Her glance swept the rest of the class. "Let's not just limit this to written reports. Include any photographs you might have or, like Buddy, use video cameras or audio tapes. We can share the results in class."

When the bell rang, Buddy quickly learned his suggestion was not popular with the rest of the kids. Ron came over and punched him in the shoulder. "Thanks a heap, Professor."

"What? What did I do?"

"All we were going to have to turn in was a stupid report, and now Miss Danardo wants a multimedia show. All because you got a camcorder. A big, clunky camcorder."

Zekie came up to him, wearing a frown instead of his usual dumb grin. "I don't have a camcorder. I'm going to have to dig around in my dirty old basement looking for pictures. There's spiders down there, for cripes sake."

Even Tiffany Raphael, who guarded her popularity by being nice to almost everyone, snapped at him. "I am not a visual person. I express myself best through writing."

Buddy had waited for two years for Tiffany to say something to him other than "Hi, Buddy." Although he was interested to learn how Tiffany best expressed herself, judging from her tone Buddy was sure it would be another two years before she spoke to him again.

Buddy lingered at his desk, gathering his books. He wasn't in a hurry to get into the hallway, where the rest of the social studies class was probably waiting to jump on him.

A waft of Miss Danardo's perfume reached his

nose before he actually turned and saw her. Had he been a dog in another life? His sense of smell was awfully keen.

"Philip, I want to thank you for that wonderful idea about videotaping and making this project more than a written presentation."

He wondered if he should confide that the rest of the class thought his idea had stunk up the room. He didn't need a good nose to know that. But Miss Danardo looked so pleased that Buddy couldn't bear to tell her that not everyone was able to see the merits of the idea.

"Is something wrong?" she asked.

"Some of the kids thought it might be a lot of work," he finally mumbled.

Miss Danardo gazed into his eyes. "Philip, there will always be people who think something is too hard. I'm glad you're not one of them."

Buddy almost floated out of the room. Miss Danardo believed in him, and he was not going to let her down. Armed with his trusty camcorder, he was going to do the best darn project she had ever seen. Finally, something had grabbed him.

Buddy's excitement lasted through the day. He

spent most of his time daydreaming about his project. It would show Buddy as the strong, clever fellow he was—or at least as he was in his own mind.

Buddy was walking home, his head down, when he felt a hard tap on his shoulder. He turned around to see Amy standing next to him, puffing slightly, out of breath.

"Oh, hi," he said with surprise.

"You're going to be taping people who know you really well, right?" Amy began without preamble.

"Yeah? So?" he asked warily.

"Well, I want to be one of the people in your personal history." Her smile wasn't very pleasant.

"You?"

"Sure. I know you really well, don't I?"

"I guess."

"So tape me." The wind whipped her straight brown hair into her face, and she pushed it impatiently aside.

"I . . ."

"Afraid of what I'll say?"

"No," he said. Yes, he thought.

"Then there shouldn't be any problem."

"Look, Amy . . ." Buddy wished he thought faster on his feet. "Well, maybe . . ."

Amy just continued to smile. "Don't forget." She turned to walk away.

"Hey, Amy?"

"What?"

"Are you going to the Halloween dance?"

The smile was gone. "Why? What's it to you?"

Buddy wasn't even sure why he had asked her. "Just wondered."

"Well, I doubt it," she snapped.

Buddy nodded. Probably a wise decision.

His conversation with Amy wiped away whatever good feelings he had about his personal history. He knew why she wanted to be part of his tape: so she could tell the world what a lily-livered worm he was. The awesome Buddy he had hoped would come into focus on the tape faded to black. Then Sharon popped into his mind along with a few choice comments she might make. Put those together with Amy's monologue, and Miss Danardo would probably wonder if Charles Manson had joined her social studies class.

He went home and headed upstairs. He could

hear voices coming out of Sharon's room. Estella! His gloom lifted, and Buddy felt his heart start beating faster. If he stopped right here, maybe he could make out what they were saying. Of course, that hadn't worked too well last time, even though on soap operas, people were always listening at doorways, and no one ever caught them. Buddy glanced over at his grandfather's picture hanging a little crookedly on the wall and decided maybe it would be better if he could think up an actual excuse to stop in his sister's room.

Sharon and Estella were talking about Sharon's date with Danny. The scene he had witnessed in the house on Saturday night had hardly made him anxious for his own dating years to begin.

Mrs. Love had persuaded Sharon to have Danny come in when he picked her up. It was more of a threat, actually. Mrs. Love told Sharon she wasn't going anywhere unless Danny came in and said hello like a gentleman.

Well, he did come in. And Buddy supposed what he mumbled might have been "Hello." He did hear the "hell" part, anyway. Buddy had to admit Mr. Love hadn't made it very easy for Danny, though. His father acted as if Danny was some guy going to the University of Chicago instead of dumb old Danny Walnut.

"So, Danny," Mr. Love had said, after he had given Danny's unwilling hand a shake, "what are you studying?"

Sharon actually groaned.

Danny shrugged.

It was like watching a car crash.

"You don't know what you're studying?" Mr. Love persisted through tight lips.

It took Danny a while. "Shop."

Mrs. Love, perhaps feeling guilty, jumped in. "Shop—that's interesting."

No one else seemed to think so.

Despite strict orders from Sharon to stay in her room and watch television, Gram wandered into the living room. "You Sharon's boyfriend?" she asked.

"We're leaving," Sharon announced. She glanced around the room, daring anyone to stop her.

"Have a good time," Mrs. Love said weakly.

"Remedial math," Danny said as he put on his gloves. "I'm taking remedial math, too."

Mrs. Love didn't bother to say that sounded

interesting. She just walked them to the door.

That was the last Buddy had heard of Sharon's date. Maybe she had told Mrs. Love how it went, but she sure hadn't told Buddy. He supposed he could go in and ask her now. He could show Estella that he was the kind of brother who took an interest in his sister's life. Trying to look confident, he knocked at the open door.

Sharon looked up, frowning. "What do you want?"

"Hi, Buddy," Estella said, with a small wave.

"Hi." Now that he was here, looking at Estella stretched out on Sharon's bed, he didn't know what to say.

"So?" Sharon asked.

"Uh, do you have a pen I could borrow?" She never would believe he was taking an interest in her life.

Sharon looked at him suspiciously, but she went to her purse and started rummaging around.

"So how's that camcorder, Buddy?" Estella asked.

"Well, I've already made one tape."

"Of my mother making a sweet potato pie." Sharon snickered.

"She's sending the tape to her sister, so she can see how my mother makes it," Buddy replied defensively.

"It's a start," Estella said.

"And I've got an even bigger project coming up."

"Gonna tape Dad fixing a flat tire?" Sharon asked, throwing him the pen.

Buddy caught it. Not very deftly, but he caught it. "No. We're doing personal histories, and Miss Danardo said I could do my interviews on tape."

"Are you going to interview me?" Sharon asked innocently.

"No."

"But, Buddy, no one knows your personal history better than I do. I helped change your diapers." She turned to Estella. "You should have seen him. He was really a scrawny little thing, so he had to go to the doctor a lot. . . ."

Buddy felt himself turn about three shades of red. He knew what was coming next: a little bit of family lore that got trotted out when someone wanted to have a laugh at his expense. Sharon was about to launch into the story of the time he had been lying naked on the doctor's table without a diaper and had sprayed everything within a foot radius, including the doctor. Oh, that would impress Estella.

"I'll return the pen." Buddy cut Sharon off. He turned to flee.

"Good luck with your personal history," Estella called.

Buddy looked back to say "Thank you," but the words stuck in his throat. Estella was sitting up now, shaking her hair a little. She looked like one of those beautiful models in a shampoo commercial. He could even hear the music welling up in the background.

He wheeled out of the room and practically ran back to his bedroom. Throwing himself on the bed, Buddy looked at the Chicago Bears poster on his wall, but all he saw was Estella. He felt hot and then cold. Now he knew what all those songs and shows and movies were talking about. The music in his head was still playing. Buddy was in love.

Chapter Five

Buddy looked around the dining room table. He would have liked to continue doing what he'd been doing for the last couple of hours. Thinking about Estella and what it would feel like to dance with her, to put his arm around her, maybe even brush his lips against hers. Not now, Buddy, he told himself. Thinking about Estella made him fly into the stratosphere, but that wasn't where he needed to be right now. He forced himself to look down at his beef stew. Beef stew congealing on his plate. What could be more down-to-earth than that?

They're your family, now talk to them, he told himself firmly. You've gotta get started. He cleared his throat. "So, I've got this project at school," Buddy said into the swallowing and silence.

More swallowing, more silence.

"Doesn't anyone want to know what it is?" Buddy asked, exasperated.

"Of course, Buddy," Mrs. Love said, looking up guiltily. "I'm sorry; I was just thinking about the car." She looked over at her husband. "The brakes are on the fritz again."

"Swell," Sharon said. "I've been sixteen for almost three months and I've only gotten to drive the car a couple of times. Now, it's going to have to go to the shop."

"We certainly hate to inconvenience you, Sharon," her father said dryly.

"Estella has her own car," Sharon informed him.

"Who's Estella?"

Sharon gave an exaggerated sigh.

"Oh, you know," Mrs. Love said. "That tall, pretty girl with the blond hair. You've seen her around here."

Mr. Love nodded. "Right. 'Stella by Starlight.'"

Buddy jerked his head in his father's direction. " 'Stella by Starlight?' What's that?"

His father speared a carrot from his salad. "An old song."

Buddy could feel his heart beat faster. There was a song called "Stella by Starlight." Perfect! He wanted to run into the living room and paw through his father's record collection and see if he could find it. He turned and saw his sister staring at him curiously.

"Weird name," he muttered.

"Stella Yanklevich lived in that apartment across the street," Gram noted. "A big horse, re-member?"

Buddy tried not to let Stella Yanklevich take the shine off "Stella by Starlight." "So, about my project," Buddy said, hoping to change the subject.

"Oh it's stupid," Sharon cut in. "It's a personal history, and he's supposed to interview us. On tape. Except he's afraid of what I'll say, so I'm out."

"You know, Sharon, you ought to be a garbage collector when you grow up," Buddy said with disgust. "You sure can trash stuff."

"Buddy's right," Mrs. Love said. "I think this sounds like a very nice project. Don't make fun of it."

Buddy sighed. Somehow hearing his mother describe the personal history as "a very nice project" made it sound worse than Sharon's "stupid."

"Who are you going to interview first?" Mrs. Love continued.

Buddy looked around the table at the possibilities. Mr. Love was soaking his bread in the leftover gravy, his grandmother was holding a napkin to her lips to cover a small burp, Sharon was glaring at him, and his mother was stifling a yawn. Waiting in the wings was Amy, ready to talk about how he had let her down. Probably Sharon and the kids in his class were right. This was a stupid project, and he had done nothing but make it harder for himself.

"Buddy?" Mrs. Love repeated. "Do you want to start with me?"

Buddy didn't want to hurt his mother's feelings, but after her sweet potato pie performance, he didn't think it would help his confidence as a filmmaker to start with her.

"I . . . I guess I'll start with Gram."

His grandmother looked at him suspiciously. "What do you want me to do?" She obviously hadn't been paying attention when Buddy was speaking. She often didn't.

Sighing, Mrs. Love tried to explain the project to her. "Remember when Buddy made that tape of me making the pie for Fan?"

Gram sniffed. She was Mr. Love's mother, and though she got along well enough with Buddy's mom, she didn't think much of Aunt Fan. "Like she needs to eat more pies."

Mrs. Love ignored that. "Well, Buddy wants to interview you while he's taping you with the new camera."

"What about?" Gram asked. She seemed a little interested.

"Just stuff. Like what you remember about me when I was little," Buddy said.

"You cried. All the time, you cried. We had to stick a rubber nipple in your mouth to keep you quiet."

Buddy could tell it was going to take all his skill as interviewer to make sure that his grandmother didn't humiliate him.

"So will you do it?"

"If I have the time."

Why did everyone in this family have to

make things so tough? It wasn't like his grand-mother's social calendar was all that full. What was the taping going to disrupt? Her trip to the butcher?

"Will you have the time tomorrow after-noon?"

"After my shows, maybe."

"Fine, fine." He could only hope that Tony on *General Hospital* pulled through his surgery; oth-erwise, his grandmother would probably cry all through their interview. It seemed like the only time his grandmother actually cried real tears was when somebody died on one of her shows.

"You don't need me, do you?" Mr. Love asked. "I mean, your mom can tell you everything you want to know."

"Lou, Buddy needs your input, too," Mrs. Love cut in. She turned to Buddy. "Of course, he'll be on your tape."

Mr. Love shrugged.

Boy, this tape idea was rotting faster than a sandwich under his bed. "Whatever," Buddy muttered.

After dinner, Buddy went over to the wooden

shelves in the living room where his father kept his records. For some reason, Mr. Love had a gripe against compact discs. He said they sounded like they were recorded in formaldehyde, that you didn't get the high highs and the low lows that you did in records. Buddy knew better than to argue this subject. Mr. Love was going to own the last record player in America if he had anything to say about it. Buddy was saving up to buy his own portable CD player.

"What are you looking for?" Mr. Love stood in the middle of the living room, frowning. He practically wanted people to wear white gloves before they touched his records.

"Uh, I was just wondering about that song, 'Stella by Starlight'?"

"Since when do you like big band music?"

Buddy flipped over a couple of records. He shrugged.

"Oh, I get it," Mr. Love said after a few seconds.

Buddy was all set to be embarrassed, but his father only commented, "I'll dig up a recording of the song."

"Thanks." Buddy quickly moved to the couch, picked up the remote control, and flicked on the television. *All in the Family* reruns, *Cosby* reruns, *I Love Lucy* reruns.

"What if our life is a television show?"

Mr. Love, who had settled in his tired plaid chair with the newspaper, didn't look up. "Our life?"

"Yeah, say everyone's life is a TV show, every day is a new episode, and it's being beamed to outer space, where aliens watch us."

"Aliens must have a lot of time on their hands." Mr. Love turned to the sports page.

Buddy flicked to a *Gilligan's Island* rerun. "My life would have pretty low ratings."

"Mine too."

"Maybe that's why we can't change anything in the past," Buddy continued. "Just like Lucy has to keep stomping those grapes, because that's the way they filmed it. Maybe . . ."

Mr. Love raised his head. "Buddy, don't you have homework?"

"Not really." But Buddy decided not to stay until his sister, mother, and grandmother joined them to have the usual family argument over what to watch. He got up, threw on a sweater, and went outside.

It was one of those October days when you could just smell the last little bit of summer. There might be some guys hanging out by the park, but Buddy didn't feel like walking over there. He kicked some leaves around and looked back at his house. It seemed like such a small house to hold so many people and all their thoughts and ideas and feelings.

"A little late for gardening, isn't it?" Amy called from across the fence.

"What are you doing here?" Buddy replied, scowling.

"Well, certainly not looking for you." Amy was silent for a moment. "I had to get out of the house," she finally admitted.

Buddy sighed. "I know the feeling."

"Sharon?" Amy's tone was almost sympathetic.

For years Buddy had complained about Sharon on their morning walks to school. When they were younger, it was Sharon hiding his *Star Wars* figures. When they were older, it was Sharon hiding his *Playboy* magazines, knowing full well that Buddy would be too embarrassed to ask anyone if they had seen them.

Sharon had also been a thorn in Amy's side.

When Amy was about ten, too old really for a sitter, but not quite old enough to be left alone, Sharon used to stay with her. Sharon was only thirteen and mostly interested in using the phone and bossing Amy around. Amy wound up more than once fixing Sharon's lunch and cleaning the house.

"Yeah, Sharon and the rest of them," Buddy muttered.

"At least you can get away from them sometimes," Amy responded. "I'm pretty much tied to the house these days. My phone's not exactly ringing off the hook with invitations."

Buddy thought back to last June, when he had learned that Amy was out. Naturally, it had been Ron who had given him the news.

"I can't believe you're still walking to school with Amy," Ron said one morning.

"Why shouldn't I?"

Ron shook his head. "Where you been living, Buddy, on another planet? The girls are mad at her. Nobody's talking to her."

"Well, I am," Buddy said boldly.

"Fine. Then pretty soon, no one will be talking to you."

That had scared Buddy. There were only a few days of school left, and Buddy had found an excuse not to walk with Amy on every one of them. She had gotten the message. After school was over, she left for camp without even a good-bye.

Buddy wanted to ask Amy what the problem was with her and the rest of the girls, but he didn't quite know how to put the sentence together. It was weird enough just talking to Amy after so long. Before he could ask, Amy broke the silence.

"So when are you taping me?" Amy asked tauntingly. "How about tomorrow?" She pulled her jacket close and hugged her arms. The wind was picking up.

"I'm interviewing my grandmother tomorrow."

"Oh, that should be exciting. When's it my turn?"

Buddy was silent.

"I get it." Amy nodded with satisfaction. "I thought you might be too chicken to do it."

"I'm just not sure who-all I want to interview."

"Well, be sure to have Ron. He'll do his best to make you look good," Amy said sarcastically.

Like Mrs. Love, Amy had never been a big

supporter of Ron's. Amy always said he was a legend in his own mind, and she saw quite clearly all the things about Ron that Buddy tried to ignore.

"I might not have Ron be in it."

"Yeah, unless Ron decides he wants to be in it."

"Ron's not my boss," Buddy said, but without much conviction.

Amy just looked at him. "When was the last time you told him you wouldn't do something?"

Instead of answering, Buddy surprised himself by saying, "If you want to be on my tape, you can, Amy."

"Really?" she asked, taken aback. "What made you change your mind?"

Buddy didn't have the faintest idea. Finally, he muttered, "You do know me pretty well, after all."

Amy nodded, looking kind of sad. "Yeah, I do."

Her voice was soft and disappointed. Buddy didn't know when he had ever felt worse.

"I'm going in," he said abruptly. "It's getting chilly."

"Yeah," Amy agreed, "it's no fun being out in the cold." And before he could move, she hurried into her house. He stood watching until the light went on in her room. Then he slowly went inside.

Buddy might not have remembered the last time he had stood up to Ron, but his next opportunity came almost immediately. The following morning Ron was out in front of the school when Buddy walked up.

"Hey, my man, Buddy. Just the dude I want to see." Buddy smelled trouble. When Ron was going to ask Buddy to do something he wouldn't want to do, he talked in a jivey kind of way.

"What?" Buddy asked warily.

"I have an idea for our Halloween costumes."

Buddy inwardly groaned. Ron had a thing about them going as a duo at Halloween. But that was when they were younger. Buddy had been Robin to Ron's Batman, Barney Rubble to his Fred Flintstone. He was surprised Ron hadn't asked him to be Minnie Mouse when Ron had dressed up like Mickey.

"Don't you think we're a little old for that?" Buddy asked. "We haven't had matching costumes for a long time."

"Yeah, but this one is such a hoot."

"Let's hear it," Buddy said with a sigh.

"You go as the Nutty Professor, and I go as Buddy Love."

"But that means I wear Coke-bottle glasses and a stupid bow tie," Buddy sputtered.

"Yeah, we might even be able to get you a pair of buck teeth." Ron laughed.

"And you wear a tight T-shirt and look cool."

"Perfect, don't you think?"

Hearing Amy's taunting voice inside his head, Buddy said, "No."

"What do you mean, no?" Ron asked with a frown.

"I don't want to look like a nerd. Who's going to want to dance with me then?"

Ron shook his head. "Hey, don't you have an imagination? We're going to be the hit of the dance. Everybody's going to want a piece of us."

"You, maybe."

"They can't all dance with me at once. Everybody else will dance with you."

Buddy looked at him doubtfully.

"Besides, if you don't go as the Nutty Professor, what will you go as—a ghost? A pirate? Bor-ing."

Actually, a pirate was what Buddy had had in mind.

"Course, if you don't want to, I can get Zekie or one of the other guys. It won't be as effective, you being Buddy Love and all, but maybe it's funnier that way. Two Buddy Loves at the dance, one dressed like a cool guy, and the other—you—in some dorky costume."

Well, Buddy could see it all now. If he didn't play along with the joke, he was going to become the butt of it. Ron would make sure that everyone knew Buddy could have been a part of his master concept but had chosen instead to be a pirate with his sister's kerchief tied around his head and a dime-store sword stuck in his pants. Ron would probably organize some sort of a contest to see who was the World's Best Buddy Love, and Buddy was pretty sure it wouldn't be him.

"So what do you say?" Ron demanded.

Buddy was determined he wasn't going to give in quickly. "I have to think about it."

"Think about it? I don't see what there is to think about."

"I told you I might have another idea."

Ron just smirked as if he could see Buddy

dressed as a lame-looking pirate right now. "Well, don't think about it too long. I've got to get someone lined up for this. It might not be all that easy to put the costume together."

Buddy nodded, defeated. He saw the future. And it had buck teeth.

Chapter Six

Buddy's grandmother sat on the couch, idly pushing her gray hair back into its bun. She had taken her apron off, but that was the only concession she made to the interview.

Buddy zoomed in. Oops! A little too close. He could see the mole on his grandmother's neck.

"So, Buddy? I haven't got all day, you know."

"Gram, I've gotta get you framed properly."

"A picture you frame. Me you just talk to, and you'd better start talking, Buddy, or I'm going to get up off this couch and put the meat loaf in the oven."

Buddy took the camera off his shoulder.

"Gram, this is my first interview. I've gotta get it right. You're making me nervous."

Gram stared at him suspiciously from under her heavy brows. "You nervous?"

"Yes."

"Well, it's all your teacher's fault. Whoever heard of a movie for homework?"

"It's a tape."

His grandmother ignored the correction and went back to fiddling with her hair. Buddy decided to try another close-up, but before he could, Sharon stuck her face in front of the camera.

"Hey!" Buddy yelled, moving out of her way. "Where did you come from?"

"Can't you take a joke?" Sharon asked, laughing.

"Sharon, Mom said you couldn't be in here while I was taping." Buddy could hear the whine in his voice.

"Oh, excuse me, Mr. Woody Allen. I know I shouldn't interrupt genius, but I thought I might see if Gram wanted to wear some makeup for her cinematic debut." She held up a tube of lipstick.

Gram shook her head so hard the hair slipped out of her bun again. "Lipstick? No, no lipstick."

Sharon's look turned positively angelic. "Don't you want to look good, Gram?"

"I look plenty good enough."

Buddy continued to fiddle with the focus. "Did you ever wear makeup, Gram?"

His grandmother frowned right into the camera. "These are the kinds of things your teacher wants to know?"

Buddy sighed. This wasn't going to be easy.

"Are you crazy?" Sharon asked. "Gram in makeup? Not with the fuss she makes about me."

Gram turned toward Sharon, offering Buddy his first profile shot. "That's how much you know," Gram said contemptuously. "When I came to America I bought a lipstick right away."

Buddy was conscious of the dead air that followed this statement. Gram had stunned him and Sharon into silence. "Why, Gram? Why a lipstick?"

"Because during the war I dreamed about two things: a good meal with meat and a little color on my face. So when I got here, first thing, I ate a hamburger and put on some lipstick."

Buddy knew he was supposed to be asking his grandmother questions about his own personal history, but this was so interesting. He had never really thought about what his grandmother's life had been like in the Old Country. About all he did know was that she had come here, met her husband, his grandfather, who had died a couple of years after Buddy's father was born, and that she had worked in a bakery when his dad was growing up. One of Mr. Love's best memories was of Gram bringing home all the broken cookies from the bakery. He would have them with milk before he went to bed.

Of course, Buddy had seen enough pictures of his dad as a boy to know that the cookies had had a downside. Little Louie Love could charitably be described as chubby. The uncharitable would have called him fat. It was funny, because now his father looked as though a strong wind could blow him over.

"Romance Red," Gram said, pursing her lips together as though she were about to put some on.

"Romance Red?" Buddy repeated.

"That was the color. The saleslady said it was Joan Crawford's color. I didn't know from Joan Crawford."

Neither did Buddy.

"But the girl said she was a movie star, so I bought it."

"So if you wore lipstick, why are you always on my case?" Sharon asked.

"I wore a little lipstick, like a movie star. You wear too much makeup, like a clown."

Sharon didn't take the comment well, but at least she didn't threaten her grandmother the way she had Buddy when he called her a clown. "Thank you very much," she said, stuffing her lipstick in her pocket. "It's so nice to know what my family thinks of me." She flounced out of the room. Buddy breathed a sigh of relief. He put down the camera.

"Want to take a break?"

"I'll break your head," his grandmother replied. "You're wasting my time, Buddy. Remember, I got a meat loaf to worry about."

"Okay, okay." He picked the camera up. For a fleeting second he wished he had a lighter camera, but he promised himself he would never even think that because of Ron. He pushed the start button. "So how did you decide to come to America, Gram?"

Her laugh was short and harsh. "I decided I didn't want to be shot."

"Shot?" Buddy asked, startled.

"Who knew? People got shot right and left. I ran away from Russia when the war started. I was lucky. I hid. I hid in barns. Once in a chicken coop."

"A chicken coop!"

His grandmother smiled a little. "I never liked chicken since. Then I ran to Italy. I helped the Americans when they came into Italy because I could speak a little English. So I was afraid if I went back to Russia, I could be in big trouble for running away or helping the Americans."

Buddy could feel his head spinning. "Were you a spy?"

"Spy, shmy. I stayed alive. I did what I did. I married your grandfather so I could come to America."

"I thought you met here."

His grandmother shook her head. "No. He was a soldier. If you marry a soldier, you can come here."

"Did you love him?" Buddy couldn't believe he was asking his grandmother about her love life, but the question just slipped out.

For the first time Gram looked embarrassed.

"I wasn't thinking too much about love, Buddy. I was thinking about coming to America. But he was good to me, your grandfather."

A photograph of his grandparents flashed through Buddy's mind. It must have been taken while his grandfather was still in the army, because he was wearing his uniform. Standing next to him was a very young Gram. Her hair was cropped short, and she was looking down. His grandfather looked happy in the picture. He was smiling.

"Why didn't you ever tell me any of this before?" Buddy asked.

Gram shrugged. "You didn't ask."

Buddy promised himself he would ask more questions later, many more, but now, he decided he'd better move ahead to his own story. "So, Gram, do you remember the day I was born?"

His grandmother thought about it. "No."

"No!" Buddy was outraged.

"Wait, give me a minute. Yah, it was hot that day."

"That's all you remember?"

"No, your father called from the hospital and said you were the ugliest baby he ever saw."

Buddy wondered if he would be able to edit the tape. He had only glanced over that chapter in his video book.

"You had the cord wrapped around your neck. It squeezed you, almost killed you. Your face was swollen up like a balloon. I think we have a picture somewhere."

"Great," Buddy muttered.

"But it went away. Then you looked like a regular baby."

His video book said that when you made a tape, you should try to keep your audience in mind and think about what they would find interesting. Maybe the kids in his class would be interested to know about his grandmother's life during the war, but so far his own was falling flat.

"Was there anything interesting about me?" Buddy asked a little desperately. "How about when I was past being a baby?"

His grandmother thought. "You spoke Russian before you spoke English."

Buddy was so surprised he almost put down the camera, but he willed himself to keep the tape running. "No one ever told me that."

Gram shrugged. "It's true. Look in your baby book. Your first word was *nyet*."

"Did you teach me Russian?" Buddy asked.

"Who else? The postman?"

"Why did you do that?"

"I didn't plan it. Your mama was working, so I took care of you. Sometimes I talked to you in English, sometimes I talked to you in Russian. You liked Russian better."

Buddy figured that his Spanish teacher would be pretty surprised to learn he was a bilingual baby. He wasn't showing much aptitude for languages at the moment.

"When did I stop speaking Russian?"

"When you went to nursery school."

Buddy had no memory of it at all. He formed the word *nyet* silently.

"Do you remember anything else?"

His grandmother smiled. It changed her face. "You were pretty when you were little."

"Oh, not pretty, Gram."

His grandmother nodded emphatically. "Pretty. Lots of curls, and fat red cheeks. Your father always wanted to cut your hair, but I wouldn't let him."

Buddy wasn't sure if he should be mad or touched that his grandmother thought so highly of his curls.

The camera was getting heavy, so he turned it off and put it down, but his grandmother didn't seem to notice.

"The other thing I remember is Sharon and you. Always together."

"No way!"

"Sharon, she always wanted to be holding you, even though she was too little," his grandmother continued. "Then, when you started walking, she was making up games and pretending to read books to you." Gram chuckled. "And tea parties, always with the tea parties. I made the tea. She made you drink tea with her bear."

Buddy was glad that he had turned off the camcorder.

"And you! You grabbed at her all the time. Didn't want to be out of her sight. Then you two started fighting," Gram continued. "Now, you don't even like each other. A brother and a sister who don't like each other." Gram shook her head.

Buddy didn't know why she should be so surprised. Hardly any of the brothers and sisters he knew liked each other. Of course, no one had a sister that was a wild, screaming maniac whose tongue was sharper than his grandmother's meat cleaver. Buddy felt he had a pretty good reason, he thought, for not liking his sister.

"The camera's off," Gram noted.

Buddy nodded.

"Meat loaf." She got up off the couch.

Buddy had so much to think about that he didn't argue. Gram put on her apron as she headed back into the kitchen. "So that's what it's like to be on a television show," Gram said. "Not too bad."

Buddy flopped down on the couch. He was exhausted. Was it from holding up the camera for so long, or from finding out that he was a Russian-speaking, tea-drinking clingy little brother?

He felt sweat beginning to form under his armpits. There was a lot of incriminating stuff on the tape. What if he couldn't edit it? He was going to be the laughingstock of the class. He knew he should look at the tape and see just what was on it, but he didn't want to right now. Next time he'd have to remember to be very careful about the questions he asked.

Suddenly, he had to get out of the house. He wanted to go somewhere, anywhere. He didn't want to go to the corner. Maybe the mall. He could go down to the sporting goods store and look at baseball jerseys.

Sharon was standing on the porch, hugging her shoulders. Just standing around looking at the dying flowers in their mother's garden was a very un-Sharon-like thing to be doing.

"So, Woody, is the show over?"

Buddy nodded.

"Where's Gram? Gone to Hollywood?"

"No. Making a meat loaf."

"Suits her talents better."

Buddy looked at her curiously. "What's wrong with you?"

Sharon glared back. "I'm sick of everyone making fun of me."

"Aw, you've heard that makeup stuff a million times before."

"Guess that's a pretty good reason to be sick of it."

Buddy tried hard to remember what it was like when he and Sharon went everywhere together. He couldn't form an image. "Sharon," he asked tentatively, "Gram said that we used to play to-gether all the time."

"Not recently."

"Well, no. When we were little. I don't re-member that, do you?"

"I used to put my dresses on you and pretend you were a doll."

"Oh, jeez." Then it was true. Buddy couldn't tell if Sharon's smile was sly or sincere. He changed the subject. "Did you know Gram was a spy or something during the war?"

"You're kidding."

"She met our grandfather when he was in the service and he brought her back here."

"A war bride?"

"Yeah, I guess that's what you call it."

"Well, which was she, a spy or a war bride?"

"Couldn't she be both?" Buddy asked.

"Hey, this is all ancient history. Who cares, anyway?"

"I just thought it was interesting," Buddy said, hurt.

"Okay, I guess it is," Sharon said more softly. "A little."

Buddy knew that was all he was going to get

from Sharon. "I'm going for a walk," he said, turning away.

"Where are you going?"

"To the sporting goods store."

Sharon didn't say anything else, so Buddy gave a halfhearted wave and walked away.

He glanced over toward Amy's house. It was dark. Maybe he shouldn't have told her she could be on the tape. If his grandmother could come up with a bunch of surprising stuff, what would Amy have to say?

Don't think about it, Buddy thought. Think about something else. But none of the thoughts that came to mind were very settling. For instance, there was that stupid Halloween dance. Ron was still hot on the idea of the two of them going as the Nutty Professor and his alter ego, Buddy Love. In order to get out of it, Buddy was going to have to come up with some other terrific costume idea for the two of them, but he didn't have a clue as to what that might be.

He fell back on his old standby, what he always thought about when he didn't want to think about his own life. Television. This afternoon, after school, he had caught a little bit of one of the talk shows. The topic had been men who were dating the women of their dreams. Sitting on the stage were four guys who looked like four guys you might see at the barber shop or at the tire store. Next to them, well, va-va-va voomski, as Zekie would have said.

Buddy had sat riveted as these gorgeous girls said the reason they had fallen in love with their boyfriends was because they were so nice, kind, and sensitive, although in one case the guy had been very rich as well.

Buddy was encouraged. Although he wasn't rich, of course, anyone could learn to be kind and sensitive. Except his sister, maybe. If there was only a way he could practice these qualities and try them out on Estella. It seemed as likely as talking Ron out of going to the dance as the Nutty Professor and Buddy Love.

Buddy could see the sporting goods store up ahead. Maybe if there were some really cool jerseys in the store, he could convince Ron to go to the party as baseball players. He brightened. It was a thought.

The shop was open. He declined the saleswoman's help and wandered through the aisles, looking at the jerseys from all the different cities, wondering if he'd ever visit any of them. He had been to Milwaukee, but that hardly counted; it was only an hour or so away.

Pulling a San Francisco cap off the shelf, Buddy put it on his head and looked dreamily off into space. There he was, stepping up to the plate, the Golden Gate bridge in the background, even though Buddy was pretty sure that the bridge was nowhere near the ballpark in real life.

Buddy was just about to go into a batting stance when he heard his name being called. He swung around, almost knocking into Estella.

Chapter Seven

Last night, before Buddy had gone to bed, his father had stuck a pair of earphones on his son's head. "'Stella by Starlight,'" Mr. Love had said, and turned on the phonograph.

Buddy had listened to the song: *"My heart and I agree, she's everything on earth to me."*

Now, as he stood here in front of Estella, the melody wafted through his head once more.

"Hi, Buddy," Estella said, her eyes twinkling just like those stars in the song.

"Hi." Say something else, he commanded himself. "So what brings you here?" There. He could take a breath. It was her turn to talk.

Estella's smile went down a few watts. "I'm

looking for a birthday present. For my father."

Buddy remembered his mother saying something about Estella's father not living with her, but he thought it might be rude to mention it. He decided just to go with the present concept. "How about a cap," Buddy suggested, "or a T-shirt?"

"He lives in St. Louis, so I thought I'd get him a Cardinals shirt. But then I thought, he can get that in St. Louis, so maybe I should get him a White Sox or Cubs shirt. But there are so many different kinds." Estella looked around with dismay.

Buddy wanted to put his arm around Estella and tell her not to worry, that he would lead her through the deep thicket of sports attire. Before he could say anything, a tall muscle-bound blond guy about nineteen, wearing a name tag that said KURT, appeared, asking, "May I help you?"

Estella looked at him and then back at Buddy. "That's okay. We can manage."

"Call me if you need me," Kurt said regretfully. He hesitated a moment, then walked away.

"I hate the way salespeople always hover, don't you?" Estella asked companionably.

"Oh, yeah," Buddy replied, profoundly grateful that Estella felt this way. "Why don't we just look at stuff? Maybe something will grab us."

Buddy knew if he lived to be as old as Gram he would never forget the next half hour, wandering around that sporting goods store with Estella. It wasn't so much what they did; anyone watching them would have said they didn't do much of anything except walk down the aisles and examine shirts and hats. But to Buddy it was as exciting and romantic as any movie. He fingered the material of the shirts, extolling the virtues of cotton and denigrating rayon. He was proud when he was able to tell Estella anecdotes about the various teams. He even made her laugh when he told her a Chicago disc jockey had once blown up a stack of disco records at White Sox Park and almost started a riot.

Buddy was having such a wonderful time that he was hoping that Estella might look at every single item in the store, but finally she picked up a Baltimore Orioles shirt and said, "My dad was born in Baltimore. I think I'll get him this."

"It's great," he told her, wanting to support her choice. "The best one in the store."

He followed her to the checkout counter, where Kurt rang up her purchase. Kurt tried to make small talk with Estella, but to Buddy's satis-faction, she ignored him.

They walked out the door together. Buddy supposed that this was the end of the road, but Estella said, "Would you like a ride home?"

"A ride?" Then Buddy recalled Sharon whin-ing about Estella's getting her own car.

She nodded and pointed to a rather boring midsize sedan, several years old, sitting in the parking lot. "I got it for my birthday. My dad got it for me." She looked down at her bag with the shirt. "Not much of a trade, I guess. Anyway, I'll drive you home unless you want to walk."

"Hey, why walk when I can ride?" Buddy trot-ted along after her to the car.

He wished it were a convertible. He wished it were a convertible and that Estella would drive him past the corner where Ron and Zekie might be standing. Hey, be thankful for this, Buddy told himself. Isn't it enough you're riding home with Estella?

"I never asked you," Estella said. "What were you shopping for today?"

Buddy told her about the Halloween dance and his thought that he might go as a baseball player.

He didn't mention Ron's idea for a costume.

"Oh, a baseball player. That's a good idea. Do you need a date for this dance?"

Buddy's heart started to pound. Was she offering?

"Or do you kids just meet at the school?"

"Just meet, I guess."

"Well, have fun," Estella said cheerfully as she pulled up in front of his house. "And thanks for all your help, Buddy. I couldn't have done it without you." Buddy practically floated up the walk. He hoped Sharon hadn't seen him get out of Estella's car. He didn't want her asking a lot of nosy questions. His time with Estella was something he wanted to keep strictly between the two of them.

After dinner, Buddy decided there was nothing on television that could compare to just lying on his bed and thinking about Estella. He had to pretend he was under the weather to get upstairs so early, and his grandmother even felt his head to see if he had a fever. Finally he escaped. Flat on his back, staring up at the crack on his ceiling, Buddy first went over every single detail of the sporting goods escapade. Twice. Then he thought about the things the talk shows didn't tell you about love. On the talk shows, everybody was always yelling about love or fighting about it. The way Buddy felt about Estella was quiet, peaceful-like. And there certainly wasn't a sitcom laugh track behind it. Buddy wondered if he had ever felt prouder than when Estella had thanked him. Her smile was so bright and sincere it had almost hurt his eyes. Buddy curled up in a little ball. Now his eyes were getting heavy. Love sure did make you tired. No one told you that either.

"Hey, Buddy."

Buddy finished putting his books into his locker and slammed it. "What, Ron?"

Ron clapped his hand on Buddy's shoulder. A bad sign. "Have you done your math?"

Sighing, Buddy opened his locker, pulled out his math homework, and handed it over to Ron.

"Thanks." Ron shoved the paper into his notebook.

"Hey! Don't wrinkle it."

Ron ignored the plea. "Hurry up. I want to head over to the video store."

This was the first Buddy had heard of a trip to the video store.

"What for?"

Ron looked at him as if Buddy should have figured it out.

"To rent *The Nutty Professor*, of course."

Buddy slammed his locker door extra hard. Now was the moment. He should just tell Ron he wanted to be a baseball player. Say baseball player, Buddy told himself, but with Ron standing there, looking exasperated, Buddy felt his courage flag. I'll tell him when we get there.

They were about a block away from the video store when who should they see coming down the street but Tiffany Raphael, with a yellow plastic Video Shack bag in her hand.

"Hi." She waved at them. Well, probably she was waving at Ron.

"Hi, Tiff," Ron called. They stopped.

"Hi, Tiffany," Buddy added. He didn't feel like she was a Tiff to him. He wondered when she had become a Tiff to Ron.

"What have you got there?" Ron asked, pointing to the bag.

"Some Madonna tapes."

"Oh, getting ready for the dance." Ron smiled at her.

"Maybe," Tiffany teased. "What's your costume going to be? You haven't said."

"I'm not going to, either," Ron answered. "It'll be a surprise."

"Can't wait," Tiffany said, fluffing out her blond hair.

Buddy felt like the wastepaper basket that was standing on the corner. No, the wastepaper basket had an actual purpose. Buddy wondered if either Ron or Tiffany would notice if he just walked away.

"We're going over to the video store, too," Ron continued. "There's a movie I want to look at for our costumes."

"Our?" Tiffany's eyes flickered over to Buddy.

For the first time, Ron looked a little uncertain. "Buddy had an idea. I might go along with it."

Oh great, Buddy thought bitterly. Now people were going to think it was his idea to get dressed up like a total dork.

"Sounds mysterious," Tiffany said.

Ron straightened up. "Yeah." He smiled. "Yeah."

"Well, don't let me keep you. I want to get

home and watch this."

"Hot, hot, hot." Ron's voice had a little leer to it.

Tiffany just smiled and walked away.

Ron watched for a few minutes, then turned back to Buddy. "That girl has great potential."

"When did you two get so friendly?" Buddy asked.

Ron shrugged. "I saw her a couple of times at McDonald's. We talked."

Buddy would have liked to ask what they talked about, but they had arrived at the video store.

"May I help you?" the clerk behind the counter asked.

"*The Nutty Professor*," Ron replied. "You got it?"

The clerk pointed Ron toward the Classic Comedies section.

"Great, it's in," Ron said, picking up the video cover with the picture of a crazy-looking Jerry Lewis pouring chemicals into a tube.

"Great," Buddy muttered. He wondered if he was going to have to steal some test tubes from the lab as part of his costume.

"I want to look for some other things," Ron said. "*Terminator*, maybe."

"Hey, why don't you go as the Terminator?" Buddy suggested. "You kind of look like Schwartzenegger," he added. Maybe flattery would get Ron to change his mind.

"Costume's too hard. Here. Pay for this." He shoved the movie at Buddy and wandered over to the Adventure aisle.

Buddy didn't know why he was stuck paying for the tape, but there was no point in arguing with Ron. He'd just come up with some elaborate reasoning that would wind up with Buddy paying anyway, so Buddy might as well just dig into his pocket and forget the jabber.

When he went to the counter, he saw that the clerk was looking at a monitor that was hooked up to what seemed to be a couple of VCRs. "What are you doing?" he asked the guy.

"Editing some tapes."

Buddy was surprised. "You do that here?"

"Sure. People bring in old home movies. We transfer them to tape. Or we can edit tapes of people's parties and weddings."

"Is it expensive?"

The guy shrugged. "Depends on how much you want done."

"I'm not sure yet."

"Well, bring the job in when you're ready. I'll give you an estimate."

As he shelled out the money for the rental, Buddy felt like the trip hadn't been in vain. At least he had found a place to edit his tape if he needed help.

"Let's go home and watch," Ron said.

"Did you get anything else?"

"Nah."

Then it was just going to be an afternoon of *The Nutty Professor.* Oh, goody. He hoped that maybe they could watch the stupid thing at Ron's house. Buddy's family got such a kick out of the movie. Especially Sharon. But when he suggested that, Ron shook his head. "It's my mother's poker game day."

"All right. We'll go to my house."

The house was blessedly empty when Buddy and Ron arrived. Even Gram wasn't home.

"Okay, I'll cue this thing up," Buddy said, taking the tape out of its box and putting it in the machine.

"Hey, hey, what about the munchies?"

Buddy trudged into the kitchen and threw some potato chips into a bowl. He was finding all this so distasteful that he didn't think he'd be able to eat any.

Buddy brought in the chips and slammed the bowl down on the coffee table. Ron already had put himself in charge of the remote control. He pressed the play button.

Buddy hadn't seen *The Nutty Professor* in a long time. It didn't seem to matter; the story was pretty direct. There was professor Julius Kelp, a skinny, goony twit; then he devises the secret formula that turns him into the cigarette-smoking, hip crooner, Buddy Love.

"Hey." Ron punched Buddy. "Do you think I can smoke at school? Buddy always has a cigarette in his hand. It's part of the costume."

But Buddy wasn't paying attention. He was staring at the screen, disbelief all over his face. There was a girl in the film who fell in love with the Nutty Professor. He had remembered that much. What he hadn't remembered was that her name was Stella.

Chapter Eight

If Buddy had thought about it, he would have realized how remarkable it was to have spent an afternoon barely hearing a word Ron said. But Buddy was too caught up in the saga of the Nutty Professor to listen to Ron's comments about how he'd slick back his hair or find the tightest pants possible for his costume.

Who cared about what kind of grease Ron was going to wear on his head when there was a girl on the screen, a beautiful blonde named Stella who by the end of the movie decided that the hip crooner was a loser and that it was the shy professor who she really loved.

Buddy took it as a sign. He had watched enough television shows on psychic phenomena to know that things that seemed accidental often were part of a grand design. What could be grander than finding out that in the whole hated Nutty Professor phenomenon there was a ray of light? And her name was Stella.

For once in his life, Buddy didn't even feel the need to take possession of the remote control. Ron did all the fast-forwarding through any parts that he considered boring. Fortunately, he didn't roll past the Stella parts.

"What a babe, hey, Buddy?" Ron said during one scene when Stella sashayed across the screen looking as though she had been poured into her evening gown.

Buddy frowned. He didn't like Ron being so vulgar about a Stella, even if this one was just a character in *The Nutty Professor.*

"Did you see the way Buddy Love laid a big old kiss on her?" Ron continued. Now Buddy grabbed the remote out of Ron's hand and flicked off the movie. "Haven't we seen enough of this? You know what you're going to wear."

"Yeah, but do you?" Ron reached over and messed up Buddy's hair.

Before Buddy could answer, Mr. Love walked in.

"Hey, Dad," Buddy said, glad for the interruption.

Mr. Love pulled off his jacket. "Hello, boys."

Ron's reply was halfway between a grunt and a hello.

"It's just us for dinner tonight, Buddy boy," Mr. Love said.

Buddy was surprised. He tried to think of the last time he and his father had had dinner together. "Where's Mom?"

"Your mother is taking your grandmother to the dentist."

"And Sharon?"

"She's going over to her friend's house for dinner. Estella."

Buddy glanced quickly over at Ron to see if he had noticed the Stella connection, but Ron, busy eating chips, was singularly uninterested in the dining arrangements of the Love family.

"I'm going to make hamburgers," Mr. Love said.

"Okay with me. Can Ron stay?"

Mr. Love shrugged and went back into the kitchen.

"Want to stay for dinner, Ron?" Buddy asked

hopefully. The thought of eating alone with his dad made Buddy nervous. Even Ron's presence would help.

"Dinner?" Ron looked up from his potato chips. "Nah. My mom's making fried chicken. It's my favorite." He stood up. "I better be getting home. Now are we all set with this costume thing?"

Buddy shrugged dispiritedly. He could think of a million reasons to answer no, but thinking them and saying them were two different things. It didn't matter. Ron took Buddy's shrug for a big, fat yes.

"Good. Glad that's settled. Don't forget to take back the tape," Ron said as he headed for the door.

"Ron . . ."

But Ron was gone.

Buddy went out to the kitchen. His father was reading a note from his mother.

"She says the hamburger patties and a salad are in the fridge. And there's frozen French fries in the freezer. You take care of that, okay? Oh, and she says we should get started on that tape of yours."

"Yeah, I guess we should," Buddy said unenthusiastically.

"Do you know what you're going to ask me?"

"I thought I'd wing it."

Mr. Love looked doubtful. But after a rather silent dinner, he settled himself on the couch, ready to begin.

Buddy got the camera ready and pushed the on button. "So, what kind of kid were you?"

Mr. Love seemed surprised at the question. "I don't know. A quiet kid. I liked to build model airplanes."

Now it was Buddy's turn to be surprised. "But you hate to fix things or fiddle around with stuff. And I never saw you do anything like build a model. You never made models with me."

"I didn't think you liked models."

Buddy didn't know if he did or didn't. Maybe he would have, if his father had suggested it.

"Now I like to listen to music in my spare time," Mr. Love continued.

"You were born here in Chicago, right?"

"Yeah. In this neighborhood. We lived in an apartment on Winona. We didn't have much money. My dad died when I was little."

For some reason that fact embarrassed Buddy.

"I know. How old were you?"

"Three," his father said quietly.

"So you don't remember him?"

"I remember him singing to me."

A memory struck Buddy. "I remember you singing to me. What was that song? It was about doggies."

Mr. Love laughed. "No. Dogies. Pronounced like 'dough.' 'Git Along, Little Dogies.' Dogies are cattle."

"You used to sing it when it was time for me to get ready for bed."

"That's right." Mr. Love seemed pleased that Buddy remembered.

"Was it . . . was it hard not having a dad?" Buddy asked.

"I didn't know any different," Mr. Love said, after he had thought about it for a while. "I guess it was harder after you and Sharon were born."

"Why?" Buddy asked with surprise.

"What did I know about being a father?" Mr. Love said gruffly. "Hey, I thought this tape was supposed to be about you."

"I'm supposed to find out about my family. And that means you and Gram."

"It was just a family, like anybody else's."

"Not exactly. How many kids have a grandmother who was a spy during World War II?"

"A spy? Did she tell you that?"

Buddy told his father what his grandmother had said.

"I didn't know that," Mr. Love said, puzzled. "I mean, I knew they met in Italy while Dad was a soldier, but I never heard that my mother was afraid to go back to Russia or that she worked as a translator."

"How could you not know that?" Buddy asked.

"There's probably plenty you don't know about your mother," Mr. Love pointed out.

Buddy vowed to find out if his mother had been a spy during the Vietnam War, but he didn't think she had.

"Ma, a spy," Mr. Love mused. "I'm gonna ask her about that. Now what do you say we go on to you?"

Buddy would have liked to talk more to his father about his life, but maybe it was better to press on.

"So what kind of a kid was I?" Buddy asked.

"Let's see. Well, you were a smart kid. You were always asking questions about stuff. Why the sky was blue and where did flowers come from. I thought you were going to grow up and be a scientist or something."

"I don't think that's going to happen."

"No, probably not."

Buddy wasn't happy with his father's ready agreement. "But I might be something else. Like a television director, maybe."

"Maybe," his father responded noncommittally.

"You don't believe me?"

"Hey, Buddy, it's not that I don't want you to do something big with your life, but it's rough out there. You have ideas when you're a kid, like you're gonna be a baseball player, and then something happens."

"What?"

"You grow up. And before you look around, you're married, and maybe you have a kid or two and you've got to get a job. And it doesn't matter whether you want to be a ball player, because nobody's gonna pay you to be a ball player. What they're going to pay you to do is be the produce manager at the grocery store."

"Did you want to be a ball player?"

Mr. Love smiled wistfully. "No. I wanted to be a saxophone player."

Buddy turned off the camera and put it down. There was something about his dad's tone that made Buddy say, "I'm sorry."

"Hey, I never could have made it on the sax. Not professionally, anyway. It's a lot better to listen to the real greats play it. That's why I have so many records." He looked at the camera. "Are we done?"

"My shoulder started hurting."

"Well, come here. Let me give it a rub."

Buddy walked over to his dad and knelt down so his father could reach his shoulder. Mr. Love kneaded his shoulder a few times. "There? Feel better?"

It did, a little. Buddy got up and said, "Yeah, thanks." He cocked his head toward the kitchen. "I think Mom and Gram are home."

There was a rustle of bags as Mrs. Love and Gram came in through the back way.

"Hello," Mrs. Love called.

Buddy wandered out into the kitchen, where

his mother was putting away groceries. "Hi. How was the dentist, Gram? Did it hurt?"

"Buddy, I have false teeth. He takes out the teeth and makes them fit better. How much could it hurt?"

If taking your teeth out of your mouth every night wasn't so gross, Buddy thought he might consider having his teeth pulled. It would beat having to brush every night and having cavities filled.

"Did you do your taping?" Mrs. Love asked.

"We started it. We didn't get too far."

"That's no good," Mrs. Love said. "So far, the only person you've interviewed is Gram. When is this project due?"

"Oh, the end of the month."

"Well, I want you to get moving on it."

Buddy sidled over to his mother. "Maybe you could do your interview with Dad. He's not saying much."

Mrs. Love sighed. "I'm not surprised. All right. Go in there and tell him I'm joining the panel."

His father had turned on the TV. "What's this?" Buddy asked, sitting down next to him.

"A show about bears."

"I didn't know you were interested in bears."

"I'm not. I lost the remote control."

Buddy fished among the couch cushions and then under the couch itself until he came up with the remote. He handed it to his dad, who switched the channel to the football game, which was just starting. "Uh, Dad, before you get too into the game, Mom says we're going to continue the taping."

"Oh, she does, does she?"

"Yes, I do." Mrs. Love marched into the living room and turned off the television. She looked around, frowning. "We'll start as soon as I straighten up."

After fluffing up the pillows, patting the afghan folded over the back of the couch, and centering the vase with the fake red roses on an end table, Mrs. Love said, "Now, we can start."

Buddy felt the now-familiar weight of the camera as he picked it up once more. "Mrs. Love, uh, Mom, could you tell us a little bit about your family and where they came from?"

"I certainly can," his mother said in a relaxed tone. Apparently, the pie-baking lesson had left her feeling like a pro in front of the camera. "I'm one of two children; there's myself and my sister Fannie. My mother grew up in New York, but her parents came from Poland."

Buddy had seen a television show about castles in Poland. "I don't suppose they were nobility?"

Mrs. Love's lips twitched. "I believe they were from the peasantry. But my father's family had been jewelry makers in Italy way back. Maybe they made rings and bracelets for the nobility."

Buddy didn't know if his mother was kidding or not. "So you were Polish on one side and Italian on the other."

"That's right. And even though both sides of my family have been in America for a while, they kept a lot of the traditions." Mrs. Love went on to explain how her family celebrated Christmas and Easter, and how on all the big holidays there were always pierogies as well as ravioli.

Now this was the kind of family stuff Miss Danardo wanted, Buddy thought.

"So how did you and Dad meet, anyway?"

Mrs. Love looked at her husband, who said, "It was at a dance, wasn't it?"

"Yes, it was." Mrs. Love looked very insulted that he didn't remember exactly. "It was at a football dance when we were juniors in high school."

Mr. Love said, "But that was just the first time, Buddy. We didn't really get to know each other until a couple of years later. One of Fannie's friends fixed us up."

"Well, at least you remember that," Mrs. Love murmured.

"Of course I do," Mr. Love said indignantly.

"So then you got married and had kids," Buddy prompted.

"That's the right order," Mrs. Love agreed.

"So," Buddy said, coming back to one of his original questions, "what was I like as a kid? Dad said I was always asking questions."

Mrs. Love nodded. "Always. You always had a question whenever I read you a book. Like where did the Cat in the Hat buy his hat?"

Something else to edit out before the video was handed in.

"You used to like to look at picture books a lot, too," his mother went on. "It's funny, but when you were very little, you watched hardly any television at all."

Buddy found that hard to believe.

"I was a big reader when I was young," his

mother continued. "I guess that's why I wound up working in a library." She turned to her husband. "What about you?"

Mr. Love shook his head. "Hey, my mother was always working at the bakery. There was no one to read me stories."

"Maybe your dad read you stories. When you were real little, I mean," Buddy explained. "You said he sang songs."

"I thought you didn't remember anything about him." Mrs. Love looked at her husband quizzically.

"I remember that."

Gram came into the room and plopped a bowl of fruit down on the coffee table.

Buddy shut off the camera. "Hey! You're messing up my shot."

"Eat some fruit. It's good for the colon."

At least he had been spared the humiliation of having his grandmother talking about intestines on tape. His father pointed to the armchair. "Ma, sit down; we have some questions to ask you."

"Me?" Gram looked at Buddy suspiciously. "I already answered a bunch of Buddy's questions."

"Well, now I have a few questions. Buddy,

turn on your camera."

When the camera started rolling again, Mr. Love took over the role of questioner. "Now what's all this about being a spy?"

Gram flicked a little lint off her dress. "Who said a crazy thing like that?"

"Buddy said you said it."

"Not exactly."

"Ma, stop pussyfooting around here. What did you do during the war?"

Gram shrugged. "I talked to this one, I talked to that one. If they gave me food, I talked more."

"So you *were* a spy!" Mr. Love said incredulously. "My own mother."

"I stayed alive, didn't I? So I could have you. If I hadn't had you, you wouldn't have had Buddy. Then he wouldn't be standing here with that camera on his shoulder." She stuck her head forward and peered right into the camera. "And I wouldn't be answering all these questions!"

Chapter Nine

The next half hour was a revelation to Buddy. Actually, one revelation led to another. Gram's revelation that she had been a spy (or a go-between, as she preferred to call it) was like taking a lid off a peanut butter jar. The smell of nuts was all over the room.

Mrs. Love admitted that she had trained for a couple of weeks as a Playboy Bunny. For a horrible second, Buddy thought his mother had been a centerfold.

"No, no." His mom laughed. "There used to be Playboy clubs where the waitresses wore rabbit ears and little black outfits with a cotton-tail."

"Oy!" Gram groaned. "My daughter-in-law dressed up as a rabbit."

"Bunny, Ma. It sounds cuter," Mr. Love said with a laugh.

"You knew?" Buddy asked his father.

"Sure."

The idea of his very own mother as a Playboy Bunny, even for a few weeks, was so bizarre that Buddy had to laugh, too.

Then Mr. Love made his own admission. One summer, when he was supposed to be working as a camp counselor up in Wisconsin, he had quit his job and spent the last month acting in a summer theater instead.

"I played a Jet in *West Side Story*."

"What's a Jet?"

"There were two gangs in the show, the Jets and the Sharks. I was a Jet." Then Mr. Love got up and sang, " 'The Jets are gonna have their day, tonight . . .' " He even danced, if you could call sliding around the floor dancing.

Buddy kept the camera running most of the time, because there were also stories about Gram growing up in a tiny village in Russia, and Mrs. Love telling about how her Italian great-grandparents had come here and started their own little jewelry store, and they all talked about what it was like growing up.

"It was easier then," Mr. Love said.

Mrs. Love agreed. "We could stay younger a lot longer."

"Why would you want to do that?" Buddy asked.

His parents just shook their heads. "Wait, Buddy," his dad said. "Someday you'll remember this as a perfect age."

Buddy tried not to let that statement get him depressed.

The family remembered a lot more about Buddy, too. Like the time he had cut his foot at the beach. It was such a deep cut that he had to get twenty-one stitches. Ten-year-old Sharon had called City Hall to complain about the dirty beaches, and then she had called the neighborhood newspaper, which sent out a photographer to take a picture of Buddy.

Sharon came in at the very end of the story.

"I had forgotten all about that," she said, surprised.

"I didn't," Buddy said. He pulled off his shoe

and sock and showed everybody the scar.

To Buddy's amazement, Sharon didn't put on her something-smells-around-here-and-it's-you face. She actually reached over and touched the scar with her finger, and when she heard what they had been doing all evening, she asked to see the tape.

She didn't make fun of it, either. "I didn't know any of this stuff," she kept saying.

Gram kept putting her apron up to her face because she couldn't stand the way she looked on television. "Fah!" she said, every time she came on the screen. Even Mr. Love looked a little bemused. "Boy, I didn't know I'd lost so much hair," he said, rubbing the top of his head.

When they were done watching, Sharon asked Buddy to turn the camcorder back on, and she told a couple of stories. She did it pleasantly, almost fondly, much to the surprise of the rest of the family.

"Buddy, are you going to be able to use all of this in your project?" his mother asked.

Buddy had been wondering about that himself. "I don't think so." He certainly didn't want the class to know that his mother had been a Bunny.

"Well, I'm glad you got it all, anyway," his mother said with a smile.

After the camera and the tape were put away, the family drifted apart. By the time Buddy got upstairs, Sharon was already in her room. Buddy wasn't sure if he should ask Sharon about her dinner with Estella, but since she was in such a good mood, he decided to chance it.

He stuck his head in her doorway. "So how was your dinner?"

Sharon, combing her hair in front of the mirror, glanced at his reflection. "It was fine."

Sharon may not have been snippy, but she wasn't going to make this easy.

"So what did you have for dinner?" Buddy asked, desperate to keep the conversation going.

"Chicken."

There was an awkward silence. Then Sharon said, "Oh, Estella told me to ask you something."

"What?"

"She wants to know if you'll make a tape of her."

Doing *anything*, Buddy said fervently to himself. Out loud he asked, "What kind of tape?"

"I think it's for her father's birthday. She said to call her."

Buddy wanted to fly to the phone, but he managed to keep his cool. "Yeah, I'll do that." Sharon murmured something, but Buddy couldn't quite make it out.

"Did you say something?" he asked.

"That tape of yours was okay."

Buddy grabbed his heart and pretended to keel over. "She liked something I did."

"Oh, get up," Sharon said crossly.

Buddy bounded up. He didn't want to show Sharon how pleased he was by her compliment, even if it was a little thin. Then he thought of something. "Do you have Estella's phone number?"

Sharon rattled it off, while Buddy tried frantically to remember it. "Are you going to call her now?"

"Well, it would be rude not to, wouldn't it? I mean, her father's birthday is probably soon."

He hurried down to the kitchen, which was empty at the moment, and dialed Estella's number. To his relief, she answered.

"This is Buddy. Buddy Love?" There was a slightly questioning inflection in his voice; he was afraid she might have forgotten she wanted him to call.

"Buddy, it's nice of you to get back to me so fast." Her voice was like liquid silver.

"What can I do you for? I mean, do for you," he corrected himself, silently cursing.

"Remember I told you about my father's birthday?"

I remember everything you ever told me. "Yes."

"Well, I thought I might make a tape to go with the shirt."

She didn't sound very happy about it, Buddy thought.

"Would that be okay?" she asked.

"Sure. We can do it anytime you want."

"Tomorrow's Saturday. I don't really have any plans."

"Me either," Buddy said happily, mentally crossing a line through his appointment with the dentist, his touch football game at the park, and his promise to his mother to rake the lawn.

"How about late afternoon?"

"Perfect," Buddy assured her. "I'll be there around four."

Buddy spent the next day in something of a daze. He didn't even care that he had to keep his dental appointment after all. He went with a silly smile on his face, so unconcerned about facing the drill that his mother asked him if he was feeling all right. Then, without even being asked, he raked the lawn, wearing his Walkman, listening to a tape of love songs he had swiped from his father. As he lifted trash bags full of leaves and moved them out to the alley, he pretended he had his arms around Estella. A fat Estella, true, but it felt good to wrap his arms around something.

He wasn't too eager to play touch football that afternoon—he would have preferred lying on his bed, staring at the ceiling, which was fast becoming his favorite pastime—but he figured the guys would squawk if he didn't show. So at two, he headed over to the park.

"Where are you going?"

He looked over his shoulder. Amy was coming out of her house. He was surprised to see how nice she looked. She was wearing a Northwestern sweatshirt over leggings that made her look older. Her hair was held back with a big bow, and with her hair off her face, her eyes looked bigger and bluer.

"To a touch football game at the park," he finally answered.

"Sounds like fun," she said a little wistfully.

"Since when? I thought you hate football."

"Anything sounds good to me at this point."

Buddy knew the right thing to do. Here was his chance to make up for his weaselly behavior. He could ask her to come along. He cleared his throat. "You could come and watch." It wasn't much of an invitation; even he realized that. Maybe Amy would say she didn't want to. Instead, she brightened, and said, "All right."

Trying to put some enthusiasm into his voice, Buddy said, "Let's get going, then."

Amy trotted alongside him as Buddy almost jogged to the park. "What's the big rush?"

"I just don't want to be late for the game."

"Who-all is going to be there?" Amy asked.

"The usual—Ron, Zekie, the rest of the guys."

Amy grabbed Buddy's arm. "Slow down."

"Okay." Buddy cooled it to a brisk walk.

"I suppose the girls are going to be there, too," Amy said.

"They usually are."

Neither one said anything else until they got to the park.

It was such a nice day that the park was full.

Parents pushed children on swings, high school kids were hanging out at the basketball court. Buddy spotted Ron and the others over in the middle of the park. "There's Tiffany and Nina and the others," he said, in case Amy hadn't seen them.

A shadow crossed Amy's face, but she stuck out her chin and said, "It's a free country. And a big park."

Why had Amy agreed to come here? Buddy felt almost mad that she had taken him up on his offer. And he was ashamed to admit that he was also worried about showing up with Amy by his side.

As if sensing his thoughts, Amy said, "Don't worry, Buddy. No one's going to know I'm here at your invitation. See you later." With that, she veered away from the playing field and headed over to a bench where she could see the game but not really be part of the action.

Buddy was relieved.

"Where you been, Nutty?" Ron asked impatiently.

Buddy glanced at his watch. "I'm only five minutes late."

"Well, let's get this game organized." Ron

turned and flashed a smile toward Tiffany. "We're going to start," he called.

She waved back.

Now Buddy got it. Ron wouldn't be so anxious to start rolling around on the grass if he didn't have an audience.

The game went on for about a half hour, then they called a break. Ron made a beeline straight for Tiffany, and Buddy followed him.

"Are you all right?" Tiffany asked Ron, concerned. "You took some pretty good hits."

"Oh, sure," Ron said, preening a little. "I'm tough."

"You are." Tiffany giggled.

Amy suddenly appeared next to Buddy. "Gee, you're tough, too, Buddy," she whispered, imitating Tiffany's small, high voice.

Buddy stiffened. Why was Amy talking to him? She had practically promised not to.

Nina noticed Amy talking to Buddy. "What are you doing here?" she asked Amy, sneering.

"I didn't just disappear off the face of the earth, you know."

"Apparently not." Nina turned away from her and began talking to a girl named Ellen.

"Boy, they make me mad," Amy said. She was talking to Buddy, but looking in Nina's direction.

This was getting worse and worse. Amy was going to get them both into trouble.

Nina turned back to her. "What did you say?"

"Do you care?" Amy countered.

"I just don't like people talking behind my back. Of course, I guess that's what I'd expect from you."

Ellen broke in saying, "You're really polluting the park."

Amy's face sagged a little.

"No one wants you here," Ellen continued.

Amy looked around the group of boys and girls now intently watching the scene. Then her eyes focused on Buddy. The pleading in her eyes reminded Buddy of a puppy that knew it was headed to the vet's for a shot.

"She can stay if she wants to," Buddy said. It came out a little squeaky, but at least it came.

Everyone got quiet and looked at Buddy.

"Well, it's a free country," he said, repeating Amy's words.

"Hey, Buddy, what's with you?" Ron asked with a frown. "You taking her side?"

Before Buddy could say anything, Amy cut in. "Oh, who wants to stay here? Maybe this park is polluted." Without a backward glance, she stomped off.

The laughter and chatter started up as soon as Amy was out of earshot. Buddy wanted to tell everyone—the girls and the boys—to cut it out, but he was still a little weak in the knees from his few squeaky comments. Finally, Zekie asked if they were going to play anymore.

"I'm not," Buddy announced. He was tired of the park. Besides, he wanted time to have a shower before going to Estella's. On his walk back, he tried to keep his mind strictly on Estella, especially when he passed Amy's house.

After a quick shower, Buddy stood in front of his closet, just looking. He had seen Sharon do this many times, but he never thought it would happen to him. What should he wear?

He didn't want to dress up, of course, but most of his shirts were about a size too small. He had been growing lately. Finally, he put on his best jeans and the sweater Aunt Fan had given him for his birthday. He hoped it made him look preppie.

After grabbing his camera, he headed over to Estella's. Now, he was trying to think about anything but her, because if he thought about Estella, he'd have to think about what he was going to say and how he was going to tape her without doing anything stupid, like taping the whole thing and then noticing he had forgotten to press the on button.

Well, there's her house, Buddy thought, as he stood on the corner. Taking a deep breath, he went up to the front door and rang the bell.

Chapter Ten

Estella opened the door. "Come in."

She looked so pretty, Buddy thought. She was wearing a flowered dress and a locket around her neck, and her hair was loose, hanging past her shoulders. She reminded him of a warm summer wind.

He stumbled over the step as he came inside, but quickly righted himself. "Nice house," Buddy said, before he really had a chance to look around. It was bigger than his house, but maybe it only seemed that way because there was less furniture and fewer people to leave junk around.

"Thank you. I thought maybe we should film this in my bedroom."

Oh jeez. Buddy could feel parts of him begin to flutter. He didn't bother to make the correction that it was tape, not film.

"We'll check the light up there," Buddy replied. He didn't want to seem too anxious.

"Okay. Oh, I should have asked you if you want a cola or something."

"No, that's all right. I'm here to work," he said, afraid he might knock it over on her bed.

Estella looked as if she was trying to hide a smile. "You could still have something to drink."

Buddy just shook his head.

"Well, here it is," Estella said, leading him into the bedroom. "I thought I might sit on that chair."

Her bedroom was as pretty as she was. Lots of pink and ruffles and stuffed animals. Buddy felt both horribly shy and terribly proud to be there.

"So what do you think?"

"Huh?"

Estella had arranged herself in a soft armchair near the window. "How do you think this looks?"

Buddy got his camcorder and focused. Catching Estella in the viewfinder made her seem like she was his alone, at least for a little while. "This is a good spot."

"I hope it was okay that I asked you to do this."

Buddy put the camcorder down. "I like making tapes."

"I was getting ready to send the jersey, and it didn't seem like enough. I tried to write a letter, but . . ."

"I'm not very good at writing either."

Estella's smile was small. "Maybe talking will be easier."

"Are you ready?" Buddy asked.

"I guess. Oh, Buddy, can we just stop the tape if I goof things up?"

"Sure."

"Then go ahead." Estella looked more like she was going in front of a firing squad than in front of a video camera.

Buddy pointed his finger at her, and Estella licked her lips and began. "Hi, Daddy, Happy Birthday. I wish I could be there with you, but since I can't, I thought it would be fun for you to get this tape." Estella stopped, and Buddy stopped taping.

"I don't know what else to say."

"What do you want to say?"

Estella shrugged.

"But you must have had some idea."

"I want to tell him I miss him," Estella said slowly.

Buddy lifted the camera to his shoulder. "Okay. So tell him."

Obediently, Estella settled back into her chair. She certainly took direction better than his family did.

"Anyway, Dad, I'm sorry our vacation didn't work out this summer. I would have liked to have seen you."

Estella got up and started pacing.

Buddy wasn't certain whether she wanted this on tape or not. "Should I keep this running?"

"Oh, turn it off." Estella's face took on a despairing look. "This was a bad idea, Buddy. I'm sorry."

He didn't know what to say. Finally, he ventured, "What's wrong, exactly?"

Estella sat on the bed. "It's so hard. I was going to visit him, but at the last minute his stepdaughter had to have an appendectomy, so it was a bad time to come. I understand that, but it seems like there's something always getting in the way of us seeing each other. Nothing's the same since my parents got their divorce." She threw up her hands. "I'm just rambling."

But what great rambling, Buddy thought. He felt really close to her. "It's okay."

Estella looked at him pleadingly. "So what do you think I should tell him?"

"Tell him what you just told me."

"But I might hurt his feelings."

"He'd be glad to know you missed him. I saw this talk show, I think it was *Donahue*. It might have been *Oprah*. But, anyway, it was about fathers and daughters who hadn't seen each other in years, and all the dads were really sad that they hadn't paid much attention to their daughters. One of the guys cried."

"I don't think my father cries."

"You wouldn't have thought this guy would have cried either. He looked like a Hell's Angel."

Estella finally smiled. "That must have been something."

"It was. He had to take a Kleenex out of his leather jacket."

"Do you tell your father everything?"

Buddy had to shake his head. "Hardly anything. But I wish I could tell him more. It might be easier if I could tell him stuff on tape."

"I don't want to waste your time, Buddy; maybe we should . . ."

"No, no, you're not wasting my time."

Estella wavered for a minute, then went back to the chair. "All right. One more time."

Readjusting the camcorder, Buddy said, "Okay, start."

Estella cleared her throat. "I miss you really a lot, Dad. It's hard not having you around all the time. I think it keeps getting harder. I'm planning to come out at Christmas, and I hope nothing happens to mess it up. We don't see each other enough."

There were tears in her eyes. Buddy wondered if Estella's dad would notice them.

"Anyway, Happy Birthday, Dad. I hope you like your present. Buddy—he's the boy that's filming this—he helped me pick it out. Call me when you get it and tell me if you like it. 'Bye, Daddy." Her smile looked more genuine now. "Love you."

Buddy turned off the camcorder and sat down on the bed.

Estella let out a small sigh. "That's over. Did I sound like a total dope?"

"No. You sounded great." You looked even better, he added silently.

"Well, I think I said everything I wanted to."

"I think your dad's going to like it."

Estella thought about that for a few seconds. "It's funny, but I'm not even sure if that's what I care about. I just wanted to say those things, and now I did."

Clearing his throat, Buddy said, "I admire you for that, Estella."

"You do?"

Was she going to laugh? No, she was just looking at him curiously.

"I hardly ever say what I want to," he admitted. "Or do what I want."

"Oh, that's probably not true."

He thought about Ron, and he thought about Amy. "I'm afraid it is."

Estella walked over to him and put her arm around his shoulder. "I admire you, Buddy."

"Me?" he said in a strangled voice. He was conscious of her arm, but it was as if a butterfly had alighted on him.

"You're a very real person."

"Isn't everybody real?"

Estella shook her head.

"Oh. I thought they were."

They sat there for a few seconds more. Buddy was sure they were the happiest seconds of his life.

Buddy wasn't certain how he made his way home. All he knew was that after he said good-bye to Estella, the next thing he knew, he was standing in his front hall. He knew he was home, though, because he could hear Sharon shrieking at their mother from her bedroom.

"Mom, where's my red sweater?"

Mrs. Love came out of the kitchen. "You told me to take it to the cleaners."

"But I need to wear it tonight," Sharon wailed.

Mrs. Love looked at her watch and sighed. "It's closed now."

The door to Sharon's room slammed.

"What's so important about tonight?" Buddy asked, as he followed his mother into the kitchen.

"A date with Danny." Mrs. Love put on the teakettle. "You're not planning on dating anytime soon, are you?"

Startled, Buddy replied, "Not exactly."

Mrs. Love didn't seem to hear his answer. "Two teenagers at one time," she murmured. "What could your father and I have been thinking of?"

Buddy pulled a Coke from the refrigerator. His mom said stuff like this all the time lately. "What's for dinner?" he asked.

"You're on your own unless you want to come with us. Your dad and Gram and I are going over to Cousin Harold's for dinner."

Going to Harold's was right up there with cleaning out the fish tank. "No thanks."

"Maybe you'd like some company."

Buddy looked at his mother suspiciously.

"Why don't you call Amy?" Mrs. Love said casually. "Her mother told me what a hard time she's been having. And you two were always such good friends."

A few days ago Buddy would have just refused. But he had been wondering how Amy was doing after her ordeal at the park. Besides, he had promised that she could be on his tape. "Yeah, I'll call."

He waited until his mother was out of the

kitchen, and then he called. When she answered, he said without preamble, "How you doin'?"

"Oh, hi, Buddy. Do you mean did I survive my afternoon? Yeah, I'm alive."

"Those girls had a lot of nerve."

"So what else is new? Hey, thanks for sticking up for me."

"It was nothing."

"No," she corrected, "it was something."

"My parents are going out tonight. Do you want to come over and do that tape?"

"You really want me to? Okay. I guess I don't have any better offers," Amy said, laughing nervously. "I'll be over in a while."

Buddy spent the next half hour lying on the couch doing one of the things he did best—worrying. He worried about the tape he had given Estella. He had told her she could play it back on her VCR, and if she had any problems with it, to call him. She hadn't called, so maybe there were no major screw-ups, but maybe she just didn't like it and was too embarrassed to tell him. Then he worried about Ron. Ron and Tiffany, Ron and the costumes, and why Ron always seemed about five steps ahead of him. He had just started worrying about Amy, and what exactly she was going to say on the tape, when she rang the doorbell.

Buddy had expected that Amy would be wearing what she'd had on at the park, but she was all dressed up. She was wearing a skirt, anyway, and a blouse with a lace collar, and if she didn't exactly look pretty like Estella, she looked sweet.

He looked down at his own T-shirt with crumbs all over it, and quickly brushed them away.

Amy seemed a little embarrassed. "I know I didn't have to wear this, but it's just been hanging in my closet, and I thought I'd like to look halfway decent on the tape."

"You look very nice," Buddy said politely.

"Thanks," Amy answered shyly. She sat down on the couch.

"So what happened after I left the park?" she asked.

"Oh, I left right after you did. There wasn't much point in staying." He decided now was a good time to ask the question that had been bothering him since last June. "Amy, you never did tell me what happened to get you in all this trouble."

Amy twisted a strand of her long brown hair.

149

Slowly, as if the words were forcing their way out of her mouth, Amy said, "Some of the girls found a letter I wrote."

"A letter?"

Amy nodded. "To my pen pal. She lives in California."

"So what did it say?"

"It was one of those days," Amy began. "You know that girl Theresa?"

"The one who wears those weird clothes?"

"She gets them at the thrift shop. Well, some of the girls sort of cornered Theresa in the bathroom and started making fun of her clothes. Nina even tugged on this hideous skirt that Theresa was wearing, like she was going to pull it off. The whole thing was nasty."

"You were there?" Buddy asked.

"I was in one of the stalls. Sort of peeking out," she admitted.

"So what does that have to do with your pen pal?"

"I wrote to her about what happened. And Nina found my letter when it fell out of my notebook. I had said some pretty bad things about all of them," Amy said, her voice low.

150

"And she told the other girls," Buddy finished for her.

Amy lifted her head. "That was it for me. I was out like a sack of yesterday's garbage." Amy shrugged. "It's okay. I'm used to it by now."

"How come you didn't tell me when it happened? I mean, there were a couple of days there when we were still walking to school . . ."

"Before you dumped me," Amy interjected. "Well, everybody else had written me off. I didn't want to add you to the list."

And then, that's just what he had done. Buddy felt about as low as a worm's belly.

Amy broke the awkward silence. "At least we're talking now."

"What are you going to do, Amy?" Buddy asked, concerned.

"What can I do? Just get through the rest of the year, I guess. My mom says if this is still going on by the time we graduate, I can go to St. Mary's."

"Really? You mean you'd skip high school with the rest of the kids?"

"It wouldn't be much of a sacrifice," Amy said dryly.

"I know. It's just . . ."

"Don't worry about it, Buddy. St. Mary's is a good school."

Buddy didn't know what to say. To be forced to change all your plans just because kids were mean to you didn't seem right. "Maybe things will get better," Buddy said uncertainly.

"Maybe. I'm not holding my breath. So where's this video camera?" Amy asked brightly, changing the subject.

Buddy went to get it. Amy was properly impressed as Buddy showed her all the special features. "You sound like you're really into this stuff."

"Yeah. It's fun. Something I'm good at. One of the few things, I guess."

Amy gave a noncommittal "Hmmm," dashing Buddy's hopes that she might disagree with him. She settled herself back on the couch.

"Try to think of a couple of nice things to say on this tape, huh?" He picked up the camcorder and turned it on. "So when did you first meet Buddy Love?"

"I met him when I moved in next door. I came in the middle of the year. Second grade. I was real shy, and I was afraid to go to school. Buddy over-heard my mother talking to his mother, and he came and found me—I was hiding in the base-ment—and he said, and I quote, 'Hey, girl, don't be afraid. I'll walk you to school.'"

Buddy groaned. "I didn't."

"You certainly did. You took me to school, and you sort of shoved me into the room, and the next day you came to pick me up again, and then we always walked to school together."

"Until this year," Buddy finished for her.

"So you didn't want everybody bugging you. I don't blame you for that. Not too much, anyway."

Buddy put down the camera. "I'm sorry, Amy." He was surprised at how easy it was to say, especially since he had thought it was going to be so hard. Amy seemed much more embarrassed than he was.

"It's okay. I understand."

The worst part for Buddy was that he knew she really did. "Uh, so what else do you remem-ber?" he asked, getting ready to tape again.

Amy had quite a memory. She remembered every goofy, funny thing they had ever done, from making Sharon's first boyfriend pay them quarters so they'd stop singing "A Hundred Bottles of Beer on the Wall" outside the living room window to the time they had tried to help Amy's mother, who was sick, and put bubble bath instead of detergent into the washer, flooding the basement.

"Boy, we sure got into trouble," Buddy said with satisfaction, when they finally stopped laughing. He put down the camera and sat down on the couch next to Amy.

She glanced over at the camcorder.

"You're not going to use any of that tape, are you?"

Buddy sobered up. "I don't think so, Amy."

Amy sighed. "Yeah. Ron would have a great time with you and me having a sleepover."

"We were only little kids."

Amy gave him a look.

Now it was Buddy's turn to sigh. "Yeah. Ron would make it sound like kiddie porn."

"Well, I'm glad I made the tape, anyway," Amy declared. "I liked remembering all the good stuff about you."

Before she could start remembering the bad stuff again, Buddy asked, "Want a Coke or something?"

"Sure," Amy said, getting up and stretching. They walked into the kitchen, and Buddy poured them both drinks. Sitting down at the table, he said, "So have you decided on a costume for the dance?"

Amy looked at him with surprise. "You gotta be kidding. After today? I'm not going. What about you?"

"Oh, I guess I'll go."

"I bet you're glad the days are over when you and Ron used to go as a duo." She did a double take when she saw the look on Buddy's face. "You're kidding! Not Batman and Robin again."

"Worse." Buddy told her the whole horrible Nutty Professor story. It felt good to finally share it with someone.

"Why did you agree to do it?" Amy asked.

"Hey, I never said I'd do it, exactly," Buddy protested.

"But you didn't refuse either."

"Not exactly."

"So that's your costume, a buck-toothed goofball in a lab coat?"

When Amy put it like that, it didn't sound like the best idea in the world. She was waiting for an answer, but before Buddy could speak, Sharon burst through the back door. "I hate males!" she shrieked, glaring at Buddy.

Sharon turned to Amy. "Don't you? Don't you hate them, too?"

"Well . . ." Amy began.

"Oh, what do you know?" Sharon said dismissively, pacing the floor. "You're too young for boys, anyway."

"Hey, what am I?" Buddy asked indignantly. "Chopped liver?"

"Yes!" Sharon snapped.

Buddy's admiration for Danny Walnut increased tenfold. Anyone who could make Sharon this mad must have something on the ball.

"What did Danny do?" Amy asked, no longer able to restrain herself.

"Do? Do?" She dramatically opened her raincoat. A huge red ooze wound its way down Sharon's white sweater.

"Did he get shot?" Buddy asked, alarmed.

"I wish," Sharon said through clenched teeth. "He was playing around with a ketchup bottle at the party. Pretending it was a machine gun, if you can believe such an infantile thing . . ."

"And the gun went off," Buddy finished for her.

"Maybe you should take the sweater off," Amy suggested. "It looks awfully sticky."

Sharon shook her head. "No way. I'm going to be like Jackie Kennedy wearing that blood-stained suit," she said dramatically.

"I don't think you'll have the world's sympathy," Amy said, trying to keep a straight face.

"Did Danny apologize?" Buddy asked.

In a strangled voice, Sharon said, "He laughed."

"Wow!" Even Amy was impressed with Danny's lack of sensitivity.

There was a loud banging at the back door. Sharon went to open it. "You!" she shouted, and tried to close the door on Danny. He was too strong though, and he pushed his way inside. "Buddy," Sharon cried, but Buddy just shrugged.

"I've got to talk to you, Sharon," Danny said, pleading, once he was firmly established in the kitchen.

"We have nothing to talk about," Sharon said frostily.

"But I didn't even apologize."

"No, you were too busy laughing!"

Danny took Sharon's arm. "Come on, let's go in the other room."

Sharon let herself be led into the living room.

There was a small window pass-through between the kitchen and living room. Very quietly, Buddy opened the shutter a crack, and he and Amy scrunched down to share the small space. As long as they didn't move around too much, they could see Sharon and Danny perfectly.

"You gotta let me explain," Danny began.

"What's there to explain?" Sharon interrupted. "It's all right here in red and white."

Big Danny shuffled his feet. "It was an accident," he said quietly. "I was making myself a turkey sandwich . . ."

"And you started goofing around, and I told you you were going to get that stupid ketchup all over something. I just didn't know it was going to be me. Then," Sharon said, her voice rising like the wind, "you laughed!"

Danny hung his head. "I know."

"How could you laugh?" Sharon demanded.

Buddy could almost see the words forming in Danny's head. It took him a while to get them out. "I . . . I felt like such a dork. I didn't know what to say. . . . I got all embarrassed . . . and then, all of a sudden . . . I was laughing." He shuddered.

"It was awful," Sharon said more quietly. "Everyone else started laughing, too."

"Sharon," Danny began, "I'm really sorry. I'll get the sweater cleaned. . . . I'll buy you a new one . . . I'm just . . . sorry."

Buddy thought that Sharon would have to be made of ice not to see that this big old doofus meant every word he was saying.

She melted. "Oh, Danny, you don't have to buy me anything."

"Yes I do. I should never have pretended that ketchup bottle was a machine gun."

"No, you shouldn't have," Buddy whispered from his hiding place, wagging a finger in Danny's direction.

"I'm turning all the money in my pig bank over to you, Sharon," Danny said.

"His pig bank." Amy stifled a giggle.

"I'm sure the sweater can be cleaned," Sharon said.

"But do you forgive me?" Danny asked. "I don't know if I'll ever forgive myself."

"Of course I forgive you, Danny Duck," Sharon said tremulously.

Buddy had to stuff his hand in his mouth to keep from laughing.

"It was just an accident," she added.

"Yeah. An accident." He cupped her face with his hairy hand.

Amy dug her elbow into Buddy's ribs.

"Ouch!"

"Shh." Amy backed away from the pass-through, and Buddy reluctantly followed. "You don't want her to catch us."

Buddy sat down at the table. "Wow, that was like a scene out of a movie. A bad one."

Amy put her hand to her forehead, and said theatrically, "Oh, my darling Danny Duck."

"I never knew a duck could own a pig," Buddy said, and they broke into chortles of laughter.

"What's so funny?" Sharon said, frowning at them as she came back into the kitchen. Danny followed her more like a puppy than a duck.

"Nothing," Buddy said innocently. "Just telling Amy about this cartoon I saw this morning. Porky Pig."

"And Daffy Duck," Amy added, trying to keep a straight face.

Sharon looked at them suspiciously, but she just pulled at Danny's hand and said, "Let's go."

"Are you going back to the party?" Amy asked. "You haven't changed your sweater."

Buddy was amazed to see his sister blush. "We're just going out for a ride. Don't forget to clean up the kitchen or Gram'll kill you."

Danny gave them a goofy smile as Sharon pulled him out the door.

Amy and Buddy burst into laughter again. They laughed so hard they were holding their sides.

When Amy finally caught her breath after a few hiccups, she said, "You know, Buddy, I wasn't sure I wanted to come over here, but it's been great."

"Yeah," Buddy agreed. They were both quite surprised.

Chapter Eleven

Miss Danardo smiled at the class.

Buddy didn't know what kind of toothpaste Miss Danardo used, but it had to be the best. He'd seen car headlights that weren't as bright as her smile.

"I'm so excited," she said, "because I've been talking to some of you about your projects. I can't wait to see them. Remember, they're all due Monday."

Buddy remembered. He had spent the last couple of days figuring out how he was going to put his interviews together, and he had finally decided that the only way was to have them professionally edited at the video store. Then he got the estimate. Buddy didn't have a pig bank like Danny, but he did have a savings account. It looked like he was almost going to clean it out.

He had told his mother she was going to have to sign a withdrawal slip for him.

Mrs. Love looked up from her book. "You know I don't like to take money out of your savings account." When she found out how much he wanted to take, she hit the roof. "No way, Buddy."

"But, Mom, I have to." He explained about the tape.

"Oh, the tape."

"It's going to be really good, Mom," Buddy said earnestly. "But there's lots of stuff on it I can't use. Stuff I've got to get edited out."

His mother looked at him. "Like maybe your mother's confession that she wore ears and a cottontail for a couple of weeks?"

"Yes, that would be one thing," he replied honestly.

"What are you going to do with the material you can't use for your report?"

Buddy had thought about this. "I want to put it on a different tape. Maybe we'll want to watch it again sometime."

Mrs. Love's face softened. "That night we were all sitting around remembering things was the best evening I've had in a while."

"Yeah, it was like that old show, *This Is Your Life*. I felt like Ralph Edwards."

"Under the circumstances, I think I'll give you most of the money. After all, we'll get to keep the tape, and it'll be something we'll treasure for years." Mrs. Love beamed at him.

Buddy was reeling. Not only was his mother going to fork over the cash, she was acting like he was presenting her with an heirloom.

Sitting here in class, he couldn't wait to get to the video store after school. Buddy was going to watch the guy edit. It should be fun.

The hours crawled by, but finally school was over. Buddy raced to his locker, threw his books in, and grabbed the tapes he had stowed there. He was about to head out when he was stopped by an all-too-familiar hand on his shoulder.

"Where you going in such a hurry, Nutty?"

"To get my tape for the project edited." Ron's hand was beginning to feel like lead.

"Oh, that's good. The video store's not too far from Uncle Funnybones."

Uncle Funnybones was a store filled with everything from flies trapped in plastic ice cubes to fake dog doo to cheap magic tricks.

"What's at Uncle Funnybones?" Buddy hadn't been in there since he had turned thirteen.

Ron gave him that familiar, what-are-you-stupid look. "The dance is in four days. Have you gotten your Coke-bottle-bottom glasses yet? Have you even thought about your buck teeth?"

Buddy sighed. He didn't know why he thought he was going to get out of this costume thing. It made him mad, though. Maybe it was Estella, maybe it was his family, maybe it was even hanging out with Amy, but he was beginning to think of himself as the new, improved Buddy Love. Yet here was Ron, tapping his foot, reminding him nothing had changed.

"I don't have all day, Buddy Boy. We'll hit Funnybones, then you can go get your video edited or whatever you do with it." He steered Buddy out the door.

Buddy tried again. "You know I'm still not sold on this idea."

"Hey, it's too late now," Ron told Buddy cheerfully. "I already showed Tiffany *The Nutty*

Professor, and she thinks the whole idea's a hoot."

Buddy stopped in his tracks. "You showed her the movie?"

"Why not?" Ron asked, pushing Buddy along once more. "After all, she's going to see us at the party; why shouldn't she see the real professor and Buddy Love?"

"I thought I was the real Buddy Love," Buddy muttered, but he wasn't all that sure anymore, and Ron wasn't listening.

Resigned, Buddy followed Ron to Uncle Funnybones, while Ron told Buddy what great progress he was making with Tiffany. Buddy was getting more depressed by the minute. Maybe a few exploding cigars *would* cheer him up.

You had to know what you wanted at Uncle Funnybones, or you'd never be able to find it. The shop was dark, almost dingy, and the toys and jokes were piled on top of counters and were spilling out of drawers. In honor of Halloween, glow-in-the-dark skeletons hung from the ceilings, and paper cats and witches decorated the walls. A fat, balding man, Uncle Funnybones himself, sat on a stool behind the counter where the cash register was. His tie, covered with hula girls, barely covered his protruding stomach. "What do you want?" he growled.

Buddy could never figure out why a guy who ran a shop dedicated to laughs was such a sourpuss.

"Fake glasses. And buck teeth."

"Glasses—sun, crazy-eyes, clear glass, bottle-bottoms—over there." Uncle Funnybones pointed a pudgy finger in one direction. "Teeth—buck, vampire, blackout, glowing—over there." He went back to reading his comic book.

They checked out the glasses first. Ron picked up a pair with hologram eyes on them. "These are cool," he said, sticking them on Buddy's nose.

"Hey, I can't see anything out of these," Buddy said, taking them off.

"Well, try these. Oh, these are good," he said approvingly. "They make your eyes look big and dopey."

"Great."

"Now, let's check out the teeth."

"No trying on teeth!" Uncle Funnybones bellowed from across the store.

Ron shrugged and picked up a pair of plastic buck teeth. "I suppose they're one size fits all."

There was something about seeing those plastic

teeth in Ron's hand. Buddy pulled himself up to his full height. He was amazed to see that he was taller than Ron. Now was the moment, he told himself. "I don't want to go to this dance as the Nutty Professor, Ron." There. He had said it.

"What are you talking about?" Ron said, examining the teeth, barely paying attention. "It's all settled."

"Not really. I am going as something else."

Ron looked up and frowned. "Like what?"

"A baseball player."

There was a second or so of silence. Then Ron's frown smoothed into a smile. "Now I know you're kidding."

"Why do you say that?"

"Because you as a ball player is a total joke. You were the only kid I ever heard of who got demoted from first baseman to utility infielder to team manager."

"The coach made me team manager because I couldn't play. That was the summer I broke my ankle."

"Tripping over your bat," Ron said triumphantly.

"So I had one bad season in Little League," Buddy said.

"Nah. You had more than one. What about the year you had the lowest batting average anyone every heard of. Like it was 101, right?"

"No. It was 156." Buddy picked up a plastic ice cube with a fly inside it.

"Hey, Buddy, when you're batting in the 100's, it doesn't much matter."

Why hadn't Buddy considered his own unremarkable baseball career when he had blurted out that he wanted to go to the dance as a baseball player? Because it was so long ago he hadn't thought anyone would remember. He should have known Ron would.

"Besides," Ron continued, "the Nutty Professor is so right on."

Buddy threw the ice cube back in its bin. "So why can't I be Buddy Love, then? I mean, I *am* Buddy Love."

"But everyone knows you as Nutty or the Professor. It just makes more sense. Besides," Ron continued, "if you think people will laugh if you show up with buck teeth and glasses, they'll be in hysterics if you come as the cool guy who gets all the girls."

Although Buddy had been mad at Ron many

times in his life, he had never showed it. Now, he was so embarrassed and frustrated and mad, the stopper blew off his bottled up feelings. "I said I don't want to go as the Professor!" Buddy practically shouted. "Get it, Ron, I don't want to!"

Ron's usual expression was a smirk. But now, his own face flushed with anger.

"It's a lousy idea," Buddy ranted on.

"Hey, Buddy, are you yelling at me?"

"So what if I am? Who cares?"

"Nobody yells at me."

"Oh yeah?" Buddy sputtered.

"You know, you've been acting weird lately. All that stuff with Amy at the park, and now this. You better think this over, Buddy. You're heading in the wrong direction. The wrong di-rection." Ron pointed his finger at Buddy, practically poking him in the chest. "If you don't want to hang with me at Halloween, maybe you don't want to hang with me at all."

Ron's threat hung in the air. Maybe Buddy had been mad moments earlier, but looking at Ron's accusing finger, he felt fear take over the space where mad used to be. "Aw, come on," Buddy finally mumbled.

"Come on what?"

"Let's just forget it."

Ron calmed down a little. "You're sure?"

"Yeah."

"You want to forget it, we'll forget it."

"Ron, I have an appointment at the video store," Buddy said, profoundly relieved to have an excuse to leave.

"Okay, okay, I think we've got everything." Ron's voice became smooth once more. They went up to the counter, and Uncle Funnybones rang up the items.

"Got some cash, Buddy?"

This was the final injustice. It was only a couple of dollars, but Buddy resented taking part of the video money his mother had given him to spend on teeth and glasses. But with Uncle Funnybones glaring at him, there wasn't much Buddy could do but dig in his pocket and hand over the cash.

"Boy, Buddy, what would you do without me?" Ron asked jovially when they were outside in chilly fall air. It was as though their fight had never happened.

"Huh?"

"I practically had to walk you over here to finish up your costume. You'd never have finished it." Ron shook his head. "You sure are Nutty. Have fun at the old video store."

Buddy stomped down the street. He didn't know who he was more disgusted with—Ron or himself.

Chapter Twelve

Buddy grasped his package close to his chest. The weather had turned nasty, and he didn't want his precious tapes to get wet. His bag of glasses and teeth stuffed in his pocket he didn't much care about. Buddy had promised himself that he wasn't going to think about Ron or his stupid costume for the rest of the afternoon, and, to his surprise, he had been able to do that, mostly because of the great time he had had while watching Jim, the guy at the video store, editing the tape.

The whole process was fascinating. Jim had used two machines, one with Buddy's tapes in it, one with a fresh tape. They had watched the interviews on a monitor, and Buddy had told Jim

173

which material he wanted transferred to the project tape. Most of it was family history—with all the stuff about holiday traditions—as well as the least embarrassing anecdotes about him. Then Jim had put all the rest of the stuff on a second tape.

Jim kept looking at Buddy as he fiddled with the tapes. "Who are these people?"

"My family." Amy was kind of like family.

"They sure are wild," Jim said.

"Yeah, they sure are," Buddy said proudly.

As he walked along with the rain dripping down his collar and ruining his shoes, a thought popped into Buddy's head. Here he had spent all his life watching television without realizing that his family was just as interesting as the characters he saw on TV. Of course, it was easier to see that after actually watching them on a television screen. His Gram was as funny as the crotchety old grandmother on *The Beverly Hillbillies*, and the rest of them had nothing on those sitcom families who were always mouthing off and then hugging each other at the end of the show. Why had he spent all that time watching other people's families when he could have just turned around and watched the Loves?

A honking horn interrupted his thoughts. "Hey," Estella called, waving to him. "Get in."

Buddy ran over to the car. "Thanks," he said. Then he looked down at the seat. "I'm getting your car all wet."

"Doesn't matter. It'll dry." Estella turned her megawatt smile on him. As far as Buddy was concerned, the sun was shining.

"I'm glad I ran into you," she continued. "I have to thank you."

"What for?"

"My dad called me as soon as he got the tape. He really liked it," she said almost shyly.

"Well of course he did," Buddy said confidently. "Did he say anything about you coming to visit?"

"Yep. Nothing's going to get in the way of our Christmas vacation." She looked at his package of tapes. "What have you got there? You're hugging it like a girlfriend."

Buddy gave what he hoped was a suave laugh. A laugh that implied that of course, the words *hug* and *girlfriend* would be in any sentence connected with him. "I was afraid it would get wet. It's those taped interviews I had to do for my school project."

"How did they turn out?" Estella asked.

"Better than I expected."

"Well, I'm sure it's great. You certainly made me look good," Estella said.

They rode along in companionable silence. Buddy didn't even feel the need to chatter away.

"Here we are," Estella said, pulling up in front of his house.

"Say, Estella?" Buddy asked. "Sometime, could I put you on my tape?"

"Your school tape?" she asked, confused.

"No. There's another tape, with all the stuff I couldn't use for school. The more private stuff. My friend Amy is on it, and my family."

"And you want me to be on it?"

"Yeah, maybe just an interview. It would keep me in practice." Buddy couldn't believe he had asked her. She must think he was crazy.

"Well, that's a compliment. Anytime, Buddy."

Buddy floated out of the car.

"Did you get to the video store?" his mother asked as he wafted through the kitchen.

"Mmmm," he answered. He headed upstairs to his room.

"Lamb shank for dinner," Gram said, as she passed him on the stairs.

176

"Mmmm." He went to his room and lay down on the bed. He was enjoying feeling good. He stretched out on his bed and thought about his project tape and how Miss Danardo would be impressed. She'd probably smile that toothpaste ad smile directly at him.

Then he thought about the other tape. It was a funny thing. No matter how good a grade he got on his project, even an A+, he knew that the tape that would really be important to him was the one he couldn't show in class. The one with all the people he was close to remembering their best stuff, their secret stuff, and laughing. It was probably good enough to be on one of those shows where people sent in their home videos. But Buddy didn't want to do that. This was just for the Loves. Let the rest of America make tapes of their own families.

"Hey, whaddya just lying there for?" Mr. Love looked down at Buddy, sprawled on the couch watching the news. Since becoming a videographer himself, Buddy had decided it was a good idea to keep up with newscasts.

"Huh?"

"Don't you have a party or something tonight?"

"Oh yeah. It's not until seven thirty."

"Well, it's six now."

"Oh."

Mr. Love sat in his chair and opened his newspaper. "Oh, P, Q, R, S, T. What do you mean Oh?"

Buddy got up and stretched. "I'm not that excited about going." The last couple of days had gone by uneventfully. Ron had not said anything more about their fight, and neither had he. It was just assumed he'd show up as the Professor.

"Why not?"

"I don't like my costume."

Mr. Love didn't bother to ask what it was. All he said was, "So don't wear it. Wear something else."

"I don't have anything else."

Mr. Love shrugged. "So don't wear a costume. Is there a law that says you have to wear a costume?"

Buddy didn't bother to answer his father. He just got up to find the jacket his dad had worn at the grocery store today. It was going to be the Professor's lab coat. Buddy knew that on

Fridays it went into the dirty clothes anyway, so he figured he would just take it out of the hamper and wear it. That way he wouldn't have to ask for it and explain why he needed it.

Buddy thought he was in luck. The jacket had not even made it to the hamper. It was flung on a chair in his parents' bedroom. But when he picked it up, Buddy noticed a big orange stain down the front.

There was no doubt about what it was. Orange juice. Sometimes when his father made the fresh-squeezed orange juice—"BURSTING WITH VITAMIN C," as the sign said—he dribbled as he poured the liquid from the juicer to the plastic bottles. Buddy held up the jacket. This was more than a dribble. It looked liked someone had bumped into Mr. Love when he was pouring. Now the jacket looked like it was bursting with vitamin C.

Disgusted, Buddy flung the jacket down on the chair. This was the last straw.

Goony glasses, buck teeth, and an orange juice-riddled jacket. It was too much. It really was. He stomped back downstairs, grabbed his coat, and went outside.

It was cold and drizzly. He passed two trick-or-treaters, a witch and her friend whose head was covered with a big cardboard box with two antenna coming out of it.

"What are you, an alien?" Buddy asked.

"A television," a muffled voice said.

Buddy looked closer. There were a couple of people drawn on the front of the box. "Good costume," he finally said. He wondered if he had a cardboard box at home. A television would be an appropriate costume for him. And it would have the advantage of covering his head.

The rain started falling a little harder, so he ducked into the convenience store. He was paying for a pack of gum when he saw Amy off in the corner, reading a magazine.

"Hey, Amy," he said, coming up to her.

Amy looked surprised. "I thought you'd be getting ready for the dance."

Buddy made a face. "I'm not sure I want to go."

"You mean you're going to leave Ron alone, Nutty-less?"

The idea of that brought a smile to Buddy's face. "Yeah. Let him explain what his costume is all about."

Amy put the magazine back in the rack. "Sure you want to chance it?"

"I thought you'd be all for me sticking it to Ron," Buddy said, surprised.

"I am, in a way. But face it, Buddy. He's not going to like it if you make him look stupid. He could turn the guys against you. Look what happened to me."

Buddy thought about it. He knew Amy was right. Heck, Ron had threatened to do just that. Still, could things be any worse than they were now? As it was, when Ron said, "Jump," Buddy had to ask, "How high?"

"What would you do if the guys wouldn't talk to you?" Amy asked, interrupting his thoughts.

Buddy smiled at her and without hesitation said, "I guess I'd have to spend more time with you."

Amy looked pleased.

"Heck, I think I'm gonna do that anyway."

"I'll be around," Amy said softly. "So what are you going to do, Buddy? About the dance, I mean."

He shrugged. "I haven't decided yet. But I'll

call you tomorrow and let you know how it all turned out."

Buddy left the store and began walking home. He knew that time was ticking by. Ron was expecting him at the gym on time, so they could walk in together.

"So everyone will get the joke right off," Ron had told him.

That was the problem. Everyone would get it. Get that he was Ron's dopey alter ego, who couldn't even hang on to his own name. Maybe he had been that person once, but he wasn't anymore. He was Buddy Love, videographer, brother, son, grandson, friend. And then Buddy knew exactly what he was going to the party as. Why hadn't he figured it out before?

A half hour later, Buddy was walking out the door to the dance.

His father looked up from his newspaper. "That's your costume?"

"Yep."

"So you took my advice."

"You were right, Dad. There's no law that says I have to get dressed up. I'm just going as myself. The real Buddy Love."

His father resumed reading. "Nothing wrong with that."

Nope, Buddy thought as he shut the door behind him. Nothing at all.